SILHOUETTE

SILHOUETTE

Paul G. Swingle

Advance praise for Paul G. Swingle's *Silhouette*:

This brilliant and deceptively simple novel allows us into the lives and hearts of two of the loneliest people ever, gazing at one another and tempting us to fear (and hope) they will never abandon the pleasures of voyeurism. What happens next is . . . well, you owe yourself the deep joy of finding out for yourself.

> James R. Kincaid, author of *Lost*, the *Wendell and Tyler* trilogy, *You Must Remember This*, and many other works of fiction

How do any of us break through the tempered and shatterproof glass we've hermetically encased ourselves inside? How do we get our arms around the tree trunk of our vulnerabilities to peel back the bark to expose our cambium delights to others? Paul Swingle's Silhouette gives us tutors in the form of Gladys and Jim, who offer up a Master Class on the artistry of leap taking.

> Michael Scott Curnes, author of *Wicked Ninnish*, *Coping with Ash*, *For the Love of Mother*, *VAL*

This novella chronicles the rich inner lives of two ordinary, lonely people. It's a poignant reminder that human connection and kindness can ease despair and improve the quality of our lives.

> Laurel Mae Hislop, author of *Chitchat, f-holes of MELANCHOLIA*, and *Deep Song: Cante Jondo*

Author Paul G. Swingle hits the ground running with this harrowing tale of depression, lone- liness, and the desperate need for connection ... you may want to reach through the page and hug these poor souls by the end.

Joshua Bligh, *Independent Book Review*

In this thought-provoking narrative, Swingle illuminates the impact of depression, offering many rich and evocative details.

Kirkus Reviews

TABLE OF CONTENTS

Chapter 1

Jim

Tonight, I saw a rooftop patio umbrella move.

Or was it a woman?

It's May 31, the night of the blue moon. I was taking my dog Gus for his nightly walk. On the rooftop of a building across the street from my apartment, against the light of the huge moon, I saw the silhouette of a patio umbrella.

I'd been seeing that umbrella on that roof for weeks—months, maybe. Every time I walked the dog or snuck a puff on my cigar, it was there. Immobile and static. Always in the same place, always visible against either the daytime sky or the city-lit night.

I had thought nothing of it, other than wondering if anyone ever used that patio.

But tonight, I saw the umbrella silhouette move.

"Son of a bitch," I said. "What the hell is that? Was it the wind?"

Startled, I tried to shake off an eerie feeling. Had the umbrella really moved? I don't care for rooftop patios myself. I've been to a few. You have to drag yourself up the stairs, hoping no one else is there when you arrive, so you can have a bit of solace. I always forget something downstairs. It's never relaxing.

The umbrella has been in the same spot, unopened, for as long as I can recall. That suggests that no one ever trudges up there. So how could the umbrella move now?

Maybe it was the wind . . . but there was no wind.

I waited, but the umbrella didn't move again.

"Come on, Gus," I said. Gus wagged his tail and we walked on. Sitting in my apartment now, I decide that what I had thought was an umbrella was actually a real person . . . a woman.

Am I going mad? Maybe the upper part of what I thought was the umbrella was actually a shawl over her head. Or maybe it was her beautiful long hair, cascading over her shoulders to her waist. She appeared slender and petite.

I wonder how old she is.

I decide that she has been watching me, and that she moved to stir my interest.

Why has she been so still until now? Why was she standing there every night, in the same bloody spot?

I'm stunned to realize my heart aches for her to move again. "You stupid old fool," I say. Here I am, like that poor old delusional Quixote, believing an umbrella is a woman, and longing for it to move. Here I am, ignoring the fact that a real person would not stand there for weeks or months, so still that I thought she was an umbrella.

"You stupid lonely jerk," I say—loud enough for Gus to cast an eye at me from his side of the room.

I wonder if the next time I see her, I should wave.

So, am I back to thinking an umbrella is a person again? I realize how empty I feel. How purposeless. And I realize that if the silhouette is a real person, how overwhelmingly lonely *she* must feel. "My God," I say. Is she up there every night, working up the courage to . . . jump? That would explain a lot.

Maybe she's one of these woo-woo types—up there meditating or channelling or whatever the hell they do.

I don't know. I still feel empty. I'm increasingly troubled by that feeling lately. I trudge through my days with little enthusiasm. I do my work well and carefully, but I don't care if it's morning or night, or if it's a weekday or weekend. And when I do have time off, I want to get back to the work week, so my day is occupied.

But this little event—this movement of the silhouette—seems to have triggered something else in me. A flood of sorrow, or discontent, or . . . I don't know, just a big empty hole. I guess that's where the term *in the pits* comes from. I'm in the pits.

Sitting in my apartment, listening to Gus snore, I recall the feeling of despair I experienced around noon today. Dawdling around in the lunchroom, a small item in some magazine caught my attention. It was about the nearest galaxies to earth. Some no-count dwarf galaxies are a mere 25,000 light years from us. One of the closest major players, Andromeda, is something like two-and-a-half million light years away.

A light year is roughly six trillion miles.

Sometimes I'm able to ponder these imponderables in a positive way, awed by the mysterious incomprehensibility of it all. At those times I think about astronomers with envy—about how they explore the magnificence of the universe, the origins of life, and other heady stuff.

But today I was just hit with a profound feeling of pointlessness. You are born, you live, and you die. And who gives a damn? The vastness of the thing is enough to make you feel insignificant.

Yet my funk reminded me of a joke I heard from one of the guys at work. A rabbi was standing in front of the "Ark," I think he called it—the box containing the Torah. Overwhelmed with piety, he fell to his knees and beat his chest, shouting, "I'm nothing, I'm nothing!" The cantor, seeing this, also dropped to his knees, and likewise shouted, "I'm nothing, I'm nothing!" The custodian of the synagogue, seeing these displays, joined both men, and also shouted, "I'm nothing, I'm nothing!" At which point, the rabbi poked the cantor and whispered, "Look who thinks he's nothing!"

I sigh and gaze at Gus, feeling a melancholy connection with him. It's probably just a stupid umbrella, I decide.

Gladys

Silly-man-with-the-hat, you have been gaping at me for weeks. I don't think you see me up here on the roof. I don't think your dog does, either. I guess no one does.

You walk so slowly, like someone with nowhere to go.

You seem so sad, silly man.

I keep calling you "silly-man-with-the-hat," but that's too impersonal. I need to give you a nice name. A kind name, and a strong name. A name that makes me feel close. A name that you would like.

How about *Bruno*?

No. Too much like a St. Bernard.

Let's see. How about *Shithead*?

That's unkind.

Silly man, are you going to rescue me from up here on the roof?

Will you catch me if I fall?

God, I can't stand this.

I could call to you. *Hey, Louie—what's your fucking name?*

Ah, never mind. I don't want to know your real name anyway. It's probably . . . *Homer*. Or *Ralph*. Boring and confining. Of course,

I should talk, with the beauty my mother laid on me! *Gladys*. I never liked that name. I've been stuck with it all my life.

No, I don't want to know your name, but I could call you . . . *John*. Simple and strong. Yes—for the time being, John.

You certainly don't move like a *Rory*, or a *Brad*, or a *Desmond*.

Maybe it's *Mohammed*, or one of those names I can't pronounce. You move like a *Henry*.

But no. I'm calling you John. That way you seem more stable, and not hesitant.

John it is.

John, will you save me? I know that's a bit much to ask—given that we have just met and haven't been formally introduced.

But things don't look good, John.

Chapter 2

Jim

Blue moons are not supposed to be blue, according to the experts at some observatory. But I don't believe them.

Blue moons *are* blue. And like the moon that sometimes turns blue, a patio umbrella can sometimes turn into a woman. It happened last night, when Silhouette materialized, like an apparition from a mist.

Part of me thought she couldn't be a person, because what person is going to be standing in the same damn spot all the time? Of course, I don't *know* she's been there all the time. I only see her when I'm out there with Gus-o, or for a smoke. And I've only really paid attention to the umbrella—the woman—when the moon was behind her.

I'm going to pay more attention now. It's dusk. In the dim light of my apartment, I turn to Gus. "Come on, Gus. Let's go for our walk, so we can smile at Silhouette."

I wonder if she'll be there? I don't remember a time when she wasn't. Getting Gus's leash, I think that I could also get my binoculars. Or maybe I could just get closer this time.

No. If she's real, she'll be like the bumper sticker that says, *Honk if you exist*. She'll reveal herself. I so want her to reveal herself. I *know* she's real!

I could wave, and maybe she'd wave back. But what if she didn't? I have so much to tell her!

Gus and I arrive on the street, and I look up.

"There she is, Gus!" I whisper.

Gladys

John, at last you've come.

Did you see the blue moon last evening? It was so huge, and blue, and still.

There you go, gaping at me. Yes, John, I'm real! Should I wave at you?

You know, John, never mind—it's okay to gape. For some stupid reason I feel better when you're looking at me. Usually I feel so alone and achy in my stomach—no, higher than that. In my chest, between my breasts. But talking to you—I guess it's talking *at* you—makes that sick gut feeling ease up a bit.

It's stupid, I know. I should get a life. Or fucking end the one I have. What kind of asshole stands in one place on a rooftop patio, endlessly hoping something will change?

Stop looking at me, you fucking creep.

I'm sorry, John. I don't know what I meant by that. I don't know what to do. God, what's happened to me? There's no point.

Don't worry, John—I'd like to jump, but I won't. I couldn't do it. I just can't imagine getting past the terror enough to hurl myself over the rail. You won't have to be traumatized by my splattering myself at your feet while you're walking your fucking dog.

God, what a fucking loser I am. I'd gladly trade places with your fucking dog. What's his name, anyway? I'll call him Bowser.

Women aren't jumpers. Did you know that? We don't use guns either—at least not on ourselves. We'd shoot a prick on a moment's notice, though. Ha ha. Anyway, John—although I'd love to throw myself off this planet, it ain't going to happen.

But you never know, do you?

Sorry. Not trying to fake you out. Are you lonely, John? God, it's getting cold and miserable out here. Walk Bowser, John, so I can leave my post and get warm. I'm going to stay very still until you leave. Maybe you'll forget that I'm a real person. We can continue our chat some other night. I'm going to stay very still, so you can drift away.

Chapter 3

Jim

"Morning, Gus!" I say.

"I'm very excited, Gus-o. Today we're going to see if Silhouette is for real. What do you think?"

Gus wags his tail, ready for a walk.

It's daytime, so I think maybe we'll be able to see her face, and her hair—or shawl, if that's what it is. Or maybe we'll see that she is simply an umbrella for a rooftop patio that nobody uses.

"Oh, Gus, please let her be a real person."

I'm so anxious that I decide not to make coffee. But I feed Gus—because he's the nicest Gus-o there ever was.

Gladys

I think this is going to be the day.

Poor John never noticed me till two evenings ago. Then he saw me move.

Don't think he noticed me before that. I wonder why?

Why doesn't anyone notice me?

But why *would* anyone notice me? I'm just a miserable piece of shit.

I think I'll wave to him this morning. No—*he* should wave. But he won't. Why would he?

He'd notice me if I splattered.

Would he even care? I bet he wouldn't give a shit.

God, why such misery?

Is it me? What have I done?

It must be me—I stand up here like some dimwit, waiting for something to happen.

Know what they call a smart blond? A golden retriever. Well, John, I am a blond, but my hair is long and mousy. It's not sexy, or even pleasant—just unkempt. Ratty, even. It looks like I've just been in the rain.

Wait—what's that?

Well, well, well—good morning, John and Bowser.

You looked at me as soon as you came out the door. I guess that means you're interested—or at least curious. Well, well, well.

Jim

"Bloody hell, Gus," I whisper, trying not to draw attention. "It's a real live woman!"

I mustn't stare—but she's beautiful, I think. On the thirteenth—no, the fourteenth floor. About a block and a half away.

She doesn't look very tall, though it's hard to tell from here. She's not short, either. Average height, I think. And the railing

12

in front of her is, what—four foot? And she's maybe a foot and a half taller than that?

"Oh! She's looking at me, Gus—I'm sure. Should I wave?"

But I don't think I can work up the courage for that.

"Hi, Silhouette," I finally say. It's quiet on the street this morning, but I don't care if anyone else can see or hear me. "Let me introduce myself. I'm Jim. James, actually. James Paterson."

I pause, wondering if *she* can hear me.

"I'm a lawyer—not much of one, though. A real-estate lawyer. With a pretty large company. But real estate lawyers aren't big deals in law practices. Kind of low guys on the totem pole." I chuckle. "Nobody goes to law school to be a real estate lawyer! But I make a decent living."

I feel my heart racing. Have I said too much?

"Did you know that ninety-nine percent of lawyers give the others a bad name? Well, real estate lawyers are the one percent that don't give lawyers a bad name. Still, we charge far more than we should!"

That's enough. You're boring her.

"I have to get going. I'll tell you more about myself when I see you tonight. Bye, Silhouette."

I lead Gus away so he can get his business done.

Gladys

Don't go, John.

I bet if I wave, he'd stay.

John, I'm sad and lonely. Please stay and talk. I'll tell you all about myself. Not that there's much to tell.

Oh, he's going. Oh, oh, oh.

Chapter 4

Gladys

He's late.

Wonder if he's coming tonight. Maybe he'll wave. Then what?

This is so stupid. I just want to throw myself off this fucking roof. But I won't. I can't imagine doing that. The sheer sickening terror of it.

Women aren't jumpers anyway. I can see why. I just don't have the guts or the craziness to do it.

Where did I see that about jumping off buildings? If you are going to jump, you make your decision before you start up the stairs or elevator, and then just walk to the edge and do it. You don't go with the intention of pondering it—if you're uncertain, you never will. At least that's what I remember. It makes sense, too.

Funny, since meeting John, I feel better about standing here. I feel less sick when I look down. I think that's because I'm thinking less about losing it and diving over.

Ah! There he is.

Hi, John. You're late. I was thinking you were going to stand me up, given that this is now sort of like a date. Right?

Oh, I see you are sitting down on that low concrete wall in the back of your building! So, you are planning to visit for a while. That's perfect! I hope Bowser doesn't really have to go, and piss on your leg.

Anyway, I've been thinking about how women kill themselves. I've decided I'm not a jumper. Sometimes I really like the idea of a sure and fast ending, but I can't imagine what the trip down must be like. It would only take a few seconds, since I'm only on the . . . let's see . . . the fifteenth floor. It would probably only take few seconds for me to splatter on the pavement. But can you imagine what one would experience during the fall? The utter rage? The despair at the finality of the act? The suffocating terror? Maybe you pass out. No, I don't think so. At least in all the movies I've seen, the scream fades, but doesn't end till the splat.

I have heard that you can survive this, unless you do it from *really* high up. If you survive the fall, then you're even more messed up. Maybe you're a paraplegic. Maybe you have the shits for the rest of your life.

Anyway, don't worry, John. Although I want out of here, it doesn't look like jumping is my thing.

I think I'll give him a little twitch today. Maybe that will make him wave.

Why don't *I* wave! I'm such a pathetic, worthless loser.

Well, I have been hogging the discussion—and it's been a grim discussion, at that! What have you been up to today, John?

Jim

Ah, she's there! Let me sit.

15

"Hi Silhouette," I say. "I'm sorry I'm late. Had to get some stuff on the way home." I wave Gus over, and he settles down.

"The other day I was kinda down on myself about being just a real estate lawyer," I begin. "Well, at times I really enjoy it. Like today, for example. I had a young couple just getting their first house. They were excited and scared. It's a big step, buying your first place!"

I look around. The street is quiet. I can relax. I continue.

"When you're buying your first place, you're always overextended, and afraid that you're going to get yourself in financial trouble. You know—can't meet the mortgage payments because of things you can't control. Losing your job, getting sick, having some bastard screw you over with hidden loan costs, or worse. There are some real sleazebags out there!"

I pause. Can she hear me? I'll assume she can, but just in case I speak a little louder.

"I know a bit about these things because that's all I really do, you know—close on house purchases, clearing titles, that sort of thing. Anyway, the wife in this couple was the prettiest little thing—shy, and holding onto her husband's hand for dear life. Her engagement ring had the smallest diamond I've ever seen. Their finances were certainly stretched.

"The husband worked in a machine shop. He'd gone to one of those trade-school community-college kind of places. Made pretty good money, considering. But not enough. He was trying to be brave—comforting her, reassuring her that everything would be just great. He kept stroking her little hand and telling her that if anything happened, he could get overtime, or moonlight at another shop. But he was sweating, and he looked pale. I bet he felt a bit nauseous."

I close my eyes, remembering the scene. "She did some kind of clerical work, but they planned to have kids soon, and she was going to stay at home. I told her that was the greatest thing a mommy could do. She was so darn pretty that I can't understand why she wasn't pregnant already. Kinda brought tears to my eyes, seeing her comforted by her dragon-slayer, and him trying to pull off this purchase, and trying to keep his composure as the man of the house, negotiating with lawyers."

I smile.

"In any event, I really enjoyed working with this couple. I was as optimistic as I could be, and I praised them on their wise choices. They seemed to have a good agent who helped them get a decent mortgage rate. So many of these young kids get taken advantage of by banks and lenders. Banks really bother me—bunch of high school dropouts acting like they're moral pillars of society. They get these kids feeling really insecure about their finances and lock them into unfavorable mortgages.

"Real estate agents are pretty expensive, you know. Their commission rates seem high for what they do. But I must say that a good one—like the one these kids had—can save you some grief. They got a decent deal on their tiny house, and a decent rate. God, how lucky they were! So obviously in love, and supporting and comforting each other. Buying their first home—I bet she was young enough to remember playing house! Maybe today was the realization of her dreams and fantasies."

I wonder what Silhouette thinks of my story. She hasn't moved.

"Me, on the other hand—I'm just a lonely 'no count,' as my uncle used to say." I smile. "Oh, no—he never said that about *me*. But that was his expression for things that were disappointing. The term comes from fishing, I think—where a fish is so small that you can't count it as part of your day's catch."

I shouldn't end my happy story on a glum note. I decide it's time to take Gus-o on his walk. "I think I'll take my leave, my pretty Silhouette. Nighty night."

I start to get up from the wall, and—wait!

Did Silhouette move?

"Gus," I say. "Did you see that? Silhouette moved."

I'm halfway between sitting and standing. Feeling awkward and goofy, I straighten up, before sitting back down again. I'm going to keep watching Silhouette. And talking to her.

Gladys

I smile, weakly. He must have seen my slight movement. I wonder if I could get him to roll over and play dead.

I wonder, more seriously, if I should wave. Will this silly situation go anywhere? I feel my brief glimmer of anticipation fading into the familiar sense of desolation, and the vague nausea.

You're a jerk, John. You're probably more hopeless than . . . no. You're probably just a nice, lonely guy with nothing better to do than gape at a loser like me.

Jim

I'm watching Silhouette again, wondering what will happen next.

My thoughts drift to the purplish-gold clouds behind her. They reflect the colors of the sunset. I can't see the sunset from here—it is blocked by the high-rise buildings behind me.

She must be watching the sunset. She doesn't even know I exist.

I begin to feel like a dope. Sitting here hoping that something will happen. The longer I sit, the worse I feel.

I can't tell if she is watching me or the sunset. Probably the sunset. If she has noticed me, she has probably concluded that I'm a loser.

I sigh.

Clouds always remind me of Sil. Poor Sil! She was my wife. She has passed on, and I'm alone now, except for Gus-o. But I think she must be up there, watching. Not in a judgemental way—Sil was never like that. Maybe she's just helping me along a bit?

"I'm sure you think I'm pathetic, sitting here," I say softly to the memory of Sil. "But you know I never was very good at this sort of thing—meeting people, I mean."

I notice someone moving along the street. A feeble old fellow on a walker. He is being helped by a slight Filipino woman—at least I assume she's Filipino. There's something about the scene that bothers me—the man looks like he is struggling. His head is down, and he's looking at his feet, with a strained expression.

"Poor sod," I say to Gus.

There are many of these old people near my apartment. They probably live alone, or with their caretakers. Maybe there's a retirement center nearby.

Ha! What an idiotic term. *Retirement center.* It's really a warehouse for the dying. God's waiting room. Death must be a comforting notion to that old fellow, struggling with his walker.

Sometimes these old people seem okay. Their lives seem almost pleasant. Just yesterday I saw an elderly woman and her helper, and they were laughing and having a good time. The elderly woman was ahead with her walker, and she said "hello" to me as they slowly passed. Her helper was a bit behind, and simply smiled at me.

But watching this old guy struggling, I understand his expression. He's being *pulled* by his helper. He's struggling to keep up. I feel like going over and telling the woman to slow down and let him enjoy his walk. I think I know what he's feeling: fatigue, hopelessness, vulnerability, uselessness, fear. He feels that he's a *burden.*

I turn back to Silhouette and watch her for a few more moments. She's absolutely still now.

"This is goofy," I murmur. I get up for real this time, to continue my walk with Gus. "Good night, Silhouette."

19

Chapter 5

Jim

I'm in my apartment, talking to my dog. I think I've become a nutcase.

"I wonder if she's there, Gus. Come on—we can't keep sweet Silhouette waiting."

I pause, holding Gus's leash.

"Gus, you're a bright fellow—do you think I'm a nutcase? I sometimes wonder. Since Sil died, we haven't exactly been social butterflies, have we? You'd think I could at least do a little better than expect a woman who is on a rooftop some distance away to pay me any mind."

Gus just wags his tail. I leash him, and we head out of the apartment and toward the street.

"You're a wonderful dog, Gus-o, but you don't exactly contribute to stimulating discourse. Maybe you could learn how to talk. What do you say—want to give it a shot? My uncle told me a joke about a talking dog when I was a kid. The trainer asked, 'What's on top of a house?' The dog answered, 'Ruff.' The trainer asked, 'What is sandpaper like?' The dog answered, 'Ruff.' There was a third thing, but fortunately for you, old Gus, I can't remember what it was."

We're outside now. I stop. The rooftop patio is empty.

"Gus, Silhouette isn't there!"

I can't believe I can be this depressed because a woman who probably isn't even aware of my existence is not standing on a damn roof. Or should I say, a damn *ruff*?

"Gus, I am losing my marbles. Come on—let's get your business done, so I can get to work and maybe start acting like I have an elevator that goes to the top floor."

Chapter 6

Gladys

Well, you're right on time, John. Sorry I was . . .

Wait. I don't have to apologise to you—or account for my time, for that matter.

Anyway, what was your day like?

Mine? You don't want to know—at least not yet. After all, I haven't told you much about myself. In fact, I don't think I've told you anything.

I'll save my name for now—mainly because I don't like it. Maybe you have a sweet nickname or term of endearment for me?

But I can tell you that I'm Irish. I remember asking my granny about it. God, I loved that woman. She was the one person in this whole fucking world who loved me absolutely, unconditionally. No fuss, no grandstanding, no requirements, no disappointments. Just laughter, profound caring, and hugs. Boy, do I remember those hugs. No matter how sad or hurt or afraid I felt, a hug from Granny would change my world.

In any event, I asked granny how we knew we were Irish. Instead of saying the obvious—that she and her family had moved to Canada from Ireland—she said, "I guess because all the men have red noses." It wasn't till later that I discovered that she was referring to the effect of Irish whiskey.

I've often wondered about the Irish and their romance with booze. It's a real puzzle to me, because I don't like the stuff. Oh, I might have a beer or glass of wine sometimes, but the hard stuff tastes like kerosene to me. So, John, I'm a cheap date—I couldn't care less about fancy wine with dinner.

Supposedly, there is a genetic marker for vulnerability to alcoholism that has something to do with the way alcohol is metabolized. I remember hearing a lecture on the subject, and how 'the distribution of that marker is consistent with our stereotypes.' Fancy talk, huh? That was how the lecturer spoke about lushes in the various races. Can't be politically un-nice and say it like it is. The Jews make out pretty well, as I recall, with a low number or amount or strength—I forget how they measured that in the groups. The Irish and Native Americans don't make out so well. They develop more lushes.

But I don't think it has anything to do with an alcohol-metabolizing gene, for the Irish at least. No—I think it has to do with those sickeningly sad, sappy ballads, sung by those tear-jerking Irish tenors.

I heard one on the CBC this morning, in fact. It was the "Last Rose of Summer." It made me so fucking sad I almost worked up the courage to fling myself off this fucking roof.

The others affect me the same. You know—"Danny Boy," "When You and I Were Young." And so on. Every time I hear one, I feel like screaming "Shut the fuck up!" Music like that is why Irish men are lushes.

Now stay with me on this, John—lesser mortals don't have the smarts to follow this argument. Here's what I'm saying: people drink to drown pain.

Hey, John—where the hell are you going? I haven't finished my explanation of why Micks are lushes.

Okay, so I'll tell you tomorrow. Good night!

Jim

"Sweet Silhouette, I missed you this morning. I hope you're feeling okay."

Gus and I are outside the apartment again, and I ask him to sit with me so we can spend time with my Silhouette. It's a quiet evening—no elderly people around tonight.

"Last night I was going to tell you about Sil, my wife," I say. "She died, and now I am all alone."

Of course, there is more to it than that. I would really like to tell Silhouette about her, and how we were together, and how much I miss her, and that sort of thing. I decide to try, speaking softly, as Gus settles down on the pavement.

"Sil and I were comfortable together," I begin. "I suppose you might say we were boring. But we were content. I always looked forward to coming home—you know, after working all day.

"That was important to me. Once, when I was a student, I gave a ride to one of my professors. He had missed his bus, and I offered him a ride. He was a pudgy, soft-looking guy. He seemed meek. I think he got pushed around by the other professors, who were cutthroats. I was hesitant about offering him a ride, because I thought it might be awkward. We might not know what to talk about.

"But when I dropped him off, I saw this professor go to the side door of his house. It was dark, but the light from the house lit his face when the door opened. He had the happiest smile—a mesmerized look. I could tell that he was home with family he loved, and who loved him. He held his head high and stepped into his home.

"Here I was—a young kid who had assumed this professor was a wimp. But the image of that simple happy man is still vivid in my mind."

I have to stop for a moment, remembering that night. Has Silhouette heard me? I take a breath and go on.

"I was happy with Sil, too—though we never did much that was exciting. Just movies and walks. She liked ice cream. And we went to lots of concerts. We loved going to hear our symphony orchestra. People think that is boring as well—just sitting there listening to music. I like to close my eyes, so I am not distracted. The music is so rich when you shut out the visuals. I have heard people say that deafness is more difficult than blindness. I guess they are both tough to get used to."

I'm getting away from the subject. I have to focus. I want to tell Silhouette about Sil.

"Well, Sil . . . I don't think I told you about Sil's name. You might think it's short for Silvia, but it's not. It's pretty silly, actually—Sil is short for 'silly.' You see, Sil always used to say, 'Don't be silly.' Or else she'd call me silly when I teased her or brought her flowers. She meant it as a term of endearment, of course. Like 'sweetheart,' but more masculine.

"Funny how these things happen. I started calling her 'Silly,' because of how she loved that word. And 'Sil' came from that. So, she called me 'Silly' when we were having fun, and I called her 'Sil' some of the time—which is really silly, I suppose."

Speaking of silly—this conversation is getting silly. No movement from Silhouette. Has she even heard me?

"Come on, Gus—time to get on the road," I say. "Bye, my Silhouette."

Chapter 7

Gladys

Well, John. John. You're back. So, I'm going to finish my theory about why so many Micks are lushes. Sit your ass down. And tell Bowser to cross his legs till I'm through.

As I was saying when you so rudely left in the middle of my commentary last night, men drink because they can't deal with feeling any fucking thing, unless it's getting their rocks off. They drink when they are in emotional pain, and when those fucking Irish tenors sing those sickening, tear-jerking, morbid, melancholy, soppy, sad, depressing ballads. Men drink heavily to drown out the painful sadness caused by those fucking Irish tenors.

Now, the Italians have the right idea. Those deep throats sing good robust songs that make you want to fuck and drink wine—but fuck *first*. I've heard it said that an Irishman who had to choose between whiskey and pussy would pick whiskey without hesitation, every time. But if Pavarotti was belting it out, pussy would win hands down every time.

I can't stand "Somewhere Over the Rainbow," either. You know
... *Somewhere, over the rainbow, skies are blue* ... Don't make me
sing it for you. That song has depressed me, big time, ever since I
can remember. I also have trouble sitting through soppy Christmas
movies, like *It's a Good Life*—I think that's the name. You know,
the one with Jimmy Stewart and Clarence, the klutz of an angel.

God, I'm lonely, John. I honestly don't think I'm going to stick
around. I wish I could really talk to you.

I have a plan, Johnny, and I've been making it for a long time. I
don't want anything as quick as the way men do it—I want something slower, and more peaceful. Would you help me through it
if I asked? I don't have a soul to turn to. No one to help me do it.
No one to try to talk me out of it.

John, please wave or yell to me.

I think I'll move again—I'll see if he responds.

Yes! He straightened up and is looking in my direction!

John, please wave. Please, please John.

Jim

"Hi, Silhouette—blast, I'm tired."

Why am I so tired? It's not like I'm doing anything strenuous—
just sitting on my behind. Although I have heard that thinking
takes a lot of energy. Supposedly, the brain uses up over twenty
percent of our energy—and a lot more when we are thinking hard.

"I wonder how the hell they measure that," I say to Gus. "It's
not like you have an energy gauge in your skull, to tell you if you're
full or empty."

I return to my conversation with Silhouette.

"Today I helped an old couple buy an apartment—they just
sold their large house, and you know—they're downsizing, now

that the grave is approaching. How did I help them? I did the paperwork. That's my thing, you see."

I frown.

"I'm sorry to say I don't think they liked one another much. They seemed bitter and resentful. They were very pleasant to me, of course, but something about their interaction with each other was unpleasant, or disinterested. I asked them about their new apartment—you know, to make friendly conversation. She said it was small. He jumped in and said, 'Well, there are two bedrooms and a den, after all.' And she just nodded.

"She went on to say it would be fine because they had to get into a place with less maintenance. They did not really need all the space of their old home. I think she welled up a bit. He just folded his arms across his chest.

"It was such a contrast with the young kids I was telling you about the other night—the ones who so obviously cared for one another. This old couple seemed like a pair of detached souls who happened to be in the same room together. There was no empathy or comfort—though they surely needed it for this painful transition in later life.

"Sad. Bloody sad."

What else can one say about a situation like that? I don't want to bring Silhouette down, but I feel compelled to explain why I brought the subject up in the first place. "I wanted to shake those old folks," I say. "I wanted to tell them that the rest of their lives could be filled with joy and companionship and caring and mutual respect and love. Yes, even strong love! But maybe that wouldn't make a damn bit of difference."

I should talk—look at me. I'm lonely, talking to myself out here, sitting on this bloody wall, when I'm not around in my apartment and talking to Gus-o. It's delusional, really . . .

Wait—what's that?

"Damn! She moved again, Gus!"

But despite my excitement, I stop talking. I have to. Sitting on the wall, gazing at Silhouette, I'm overcome with emotion. My hands and feet are cold. I'm so cold and alone, and so desperately sad. I have to fight to keep the tears from flowing.

I fill each day with work, and I plod through it. I try to make it interesting or important . . . or at least useful. Is it? I have few friends. I work with all of them. They are nine-to-five friends. They have good laughs and jostle one another.

Evenings and weekends are the worst. I go to a movie or the odd concert once in a while. Doing that alone is different than doing it with another person. I miss doing things with another person. Even during the times you don't speak, the physical closeness of another person—a caring person—is all I need.

I do have Gus. We're comfortable enough. Gus is a kind, sweet, and undemanding fellow. He's not hard to take care of. He has little enthusiasm for chasing balls—or anything else, for that matter. But other than work, and Gus, I just read and watch a bit of TV—though I never had much use for the latter contraption. Overall, I seem to be waiting for life to pass.

I've tried to be stoic or spiritual—I don't know what I'm trying to do, but I want to be more positive about my solitude. I want to be quiet and contemplative—like the monks who sit for hours each day in meditation or prayer, or whatever it is they do. How do they do that?

I saw something once about a monk who was said to be the happiest man in the world. He was just sitting there in a fugue state, with an idiotic grin on his face. He might as well have been high, or drunk, or brain damaged. He seemed . . . megalomaniacal. Egocentric. Narcissistic. Self-absorbed.

Am I going down that road, by trying to be content in my solitude?

"Damn it, Gus-o," I say, as I refocus my attention on Silhouette. "Damn it, Damn it, Damn it. Let's get the hell out of here. I am becoming maudlin—you know what that means, Gus-o? It means a big baby has gotten caught in his pity pot."

Chapter 8

Gladys

Hello, John—how ya doin'?

As for me—I'm just standing around, not doing much of anything.

I saw one of those C-movies on TV last night. It was pretty late, and what they put on TV at that time is junk. Film noir, with deep-voiced, crooked-but-honest private eyes. In this one, it seemed like every damn time the main character went into a room there was someone sitting in a chair in the dark.

How the hell do these chair-sitters get in? That's what I always wonder. Shit, I can't even get into my own apartment half the time—always losing my damn keys. I really am a klutz—losing stuff, late on my bills, disorganized. It drives me crazy. And yet, the characters sitting in the dark somehow figure out where the private dick lives, and they're into his apartment faster than I can open a loaf of bread.

Private dick—that reminds me . . . know what they call a female cop? "Dickless Tracy." Ha ha.

So, John—how was your day? You seem weary. Are you weary, John? I sure as hell am. Weary, and tired of living, as I think the song goes.

But my weary is from sitting around. I sat on the edge of my bed and cried most of the morning, John. How fucking stupid. I just sat there and cried. People say you feel better after a 'good cry'—but what the hell is good about a cry? I don't feel better. I feel shitty and hopeless and forgotten and dumb and worthless—and nauseous.

I've read lots about depression, John, and no one talks about the nausea. I feel genuinely sick—in the head *and* in the body. The sick body feels like fear, I think—kind of a sickish feeling, high in my chest. The same feeling you have when you look over a balcony from high up.

It's hopeless, John. I'm going to do it—I just can't down the stuff. Oh, I've done my homework. I have everything I need. I should take an antidepressant to help me get on with killing myself.

Strange, isn't it? Antidepressants can increase the likelihood of suicide at first. Electroshock therapy, too. And a therapist I know also talks of increased suicide risk just after the patient starts feeling better. Given the wackos who go on killing rampages and are also on antidepressants, I guess antidepressants just lead you to want to kill—either yourself or others. I wonder if suicide bombers take antidepressants before deciding to blow themselves and others up? I've heard that Hitler was big on psychotropics.

Sometime I'll tell you my dreary life story, John. It had better be soon, given the state I was in this morning. I do feel better talking to you, though. You must be a psychoanalyst—you know, like old Sigmund. Analysts are not supposed to respond. They just repeat back what you say. Or sometimes they just sit there, so you can talk and reflect and get insight, or some fucking thing.

Shit—*that's* a job I want.

By the way, did I tell you that I used to be in health care? Yup. I was one of them "registered health care providers" who don't know shit—or give a shit, for that matter. But that, my dear John, is how I got what I need to guarantee my ultimate absence.

Ever hear of such bullshit? *Ultimate absence* is the fucking new word for *death*.

In any event, I want to just sit there and try to stay awake while some poor—no, patients of analysts have to be rich, I think—some pitiful asshole talks to a blank wall. I guess it works, but I wouldn't have the patience. I'd keep asking the stone-faced shrink, "Don't you have a fucking opinion on *anything*? I'm paying *you* to sit there and tell *me* what *I* just told *you*? Shit."

See, John? I'm saving a fortune. I'm baring my soul, and you say and do nothing. You just look in my direction every so often. You're my psychoanalyst. Hey, that's good: psycho*anal*yst. Freud made a big deal about assholes and shit.

No—the way you sit there and gape at me from time to time, I'll bet you're a good listener. Oh, God—how I would love to be loved by a listener. You would not have to say one damn thing—just be attentive and give a shit about what I'm saying.

Do you give a shit, John?

For some crazy reason, I think you do. And I bet Bowser there gives a shit, too, and listens to you. Do you have anyone besides Bowser? No, of course you don't. Why the hell would you be sitting there if you did? You're all alone, too, aren't you?

Are you going to kill yourself, too?

Maybe we can do it together. I think God will give us a special deal if we do two at once. We can't do it drunk, though. It says somewhere in the Bible that you have to meet your maker sober. Can't go out carousing and with a snoot full, I think is what it says, in so many words.

Hey, where you going? Seems like you just got here. Well, maybe I'll see you tomorrow. Or maybe not.

Bye, John. Keep safe.

Jim

"Well, hello, Silhouette," I say.

"I hope you are keeping well. Although I'm puzzled why you just keep standing there. I hope you are not thinking of doing something stupid, like jumping. You worry me."

I decide to tell her a story.

"I knew a guy once who hung out on his balcony, just like you. His name was Johnson. He was a funny guy—always joking and making people laugh, and with a very quick wit. One day, we were talking about our childhoods. Johnson said, 'I remember first grade. It was the best three years of my life.' And then the poor sot either jumped or fell. Frankly, I think he jumped."

I frown.

"Johnson was probably drunk—he did have a problem with booze. Some of us had a hard time believing that a guy that fun to be around would just go and kill himself. But I've heard that comedians are prone to serious depression. I guess being a comedian is like any other job—boring and repetitive. Maybe having fun—or looking like it—is just part of the act."

I should probably lighten the mood, but I cannot remember any jokes. I tend to tell the same joke for a few days, and then it slips my mind. I've written them down in the past, when I know I will have to talk with other people. But I always seem to forget anyway.

Ah! I think I remember one now.

"Lawyers seem to remember jokes about lawyers," I say. "I guess because they make us mad! Anyway, here's one, Silhouette: How can you tell the difference between a dead skunk and a dead lawyer in the road?" I pause. "There are skid marks in front of the skunk."

Is she laughing? I try again.

"What is the difference between a leech and a lawyer?" Another pause. "One sucks your blood and the other lives in water."

I stare at Silhouette.

"Silhouette," I say, lowering my voice. "Are you really . . . real?" I rub my chin. "I was just thinking, I have only seen you move . . . what? Two, maybe three times? Maybe you are just an umbrella on a patio roof. Maybe I am imagining that you are a real live woman. Don Quixote saw windmills as giants, and sheep as legions of mounted warriors. I am just as loony as old Don, sitting here and talking to you like you give a damn."

I turn to my dog. "What do *you* think, Gus-o?"

He opens one eye, looking at me without raising his head. He must think I'm a nutcase.

"You're just keeping an eye on me to be sure I don't forget to feed you."

I turn back to Silhouette. "Silhouette, I think my worrying about you jumping made me think of Johnson—the last person on earth I would have expected to kill himself. He even had a girlfriend! As I recall, she was pretty nice. I wonder how a person like that—a girlfriend or boyfriend—deals with the suddenness of something like suicide? One day you are joking with the person, and then, *poof*—they're gone. And you are left wondering what you did wrong. It would kill me, wondering why I did not see the signs.

"*That*, my dear Silhouette, is what is troubling me about you." I stare. She hasn't moved. "What possible reason could you have for standing up there like that? Do you have a grand view of the mountains and the sky and the sea? Are you having a spiritual awakening? Maybe it's kind of like meditation, except that you are leaning on the railing. It must be bloody uncomfortable, but maybe that's part of the meditation, as I think the Buddhists say. Moving through pain to enlightenment."

I laugh softly to myself. "Well, *I* sure have a long haul before I get enlightened. Maybe I can establish a movement. *Plodders toward Unenlightenment.* 'Are you trapped by enlightenment? Join

34

us on our chaotic journey toward complete lack of understanding!'" I sigh. "Well, I certainly hope you are on a journey toward something up there, and not just working up the gumption to climb over the railing."

Gus yawns and stands up to shake.

"Okay, Gus," I say. "I know you are getting bored. Let's go. Good night, my sweet Silhouette."

Chapter 9

Jim

Putting the key in the front door, I hesitate.

I'm sad, thinking of how it used to be when Sil was alive. Coming home had been so comforting. After work, I'd be tired, but it was a *good* tired. I'd give Sil a hug and drag myself to the bedroom to change clothes. I found that to be almost burdensome—I wanted to get on with other things. Sil, on the other hand, seemed to relish it. How could one spend so bloody much time putting on clothes? I was impatient. Sometimes I didn't even put socks on, after taking off the support socks I wore during the day—even though I knew I'd be more comfortable with socks. I just couldn't be bothered with the ordeal. Strange how we behave.

Sighing deeply, I turn the key and open the door to find Gus ready to pounce on me, tail wagging. He slobbers on my work clothes. Gus's greeting, at least, makes me happy.

Taking off my jacket, I loosen my tie and move to the bedroom to change for the evening. I think of Silhouette.

"Oh, if she were only here," I murmur. We could have a meal and listen to some music and just hold hands.

Could I strike up some kind of relationship with Silhouette?

I could wave, of course, to start the ball rolling. But I don't want to discourage her from coming to the rooftop. I don't want her to think I'm stalking her. I recall a conversation I had with Smitty, one of the attorneys in my office. He was trying to keep a stalker away from an elderly woman. He had the restraining order, but this creep just kept terrorizing the poor woman. He planned it very well. He'd watch her go into a store, and when she was about to exit, he'd be standing in the doorway, claiming he was just going to do some shopping and had no idea she was in the store. He did this at many locations—the bus stop, the video rental store, and even, according to Smitty, standing outside the confessional in her church. Cops couldn't do a thing, since these all appeared to be chance encounters, and of course there were seldom witnesses.

"Okay, Gus," I say. "I see you there. Let's get you some dinner."

I feed Gus and wait for him to finish. I scratch him behind the ears, and become aware of just how quiet it is in my apartment. Suddenly, I'm tired.

"Okay, fella, let's go," I say, fetching Gus's leash.

As we walk out the back door, I feel pleasant anticipation. I hope my Silhouette will be in her usual spot.

She is.

"Well good evening, my sweet," I say, smiling, as I take *my* usual spot on the concrete wall. "I was just telling Gus ... no I wasn't, now that I think about it. I was *thinking* about some creepy stalker who is frightening an elderly lady."

Silhouette doesn't move.

"If I wave," I say, "will you think I'm a creep? I'm not, you know—I simply would like to make your acquaintance." I frown. "Fat chance of that happening, I guess. But let me sit awhile and we can chat."

I think for a moment. "Let's see—what shall we talk about tonight? The meaning of life? What it's all about? God's dark side? Salvation?" I smile again. "Afraid not, my dear—I only have a few minutes tonight. I haven't eaten yet, and I'm just plain worn out. Those weighty topics require at least fifteen minutes each.

"But here's something. On my way to work this morning I watched some kids on their skateboards. Man, oh man—those kids were good! They were having a great time—turning and jumping and running their boards on the edge of the cement walls."

I shrugged sadly. "Strange how we lose the urge to do dangerous, thrilling things. Well, I guess I can't speak for others, but I know I have lost it. When I was ten or so, my friends and I used to play in an old unfinished building. There was a gap in the floor where the stairs were supposed to be. It was probably only three feet across, but to us it seemed so wide. Well, all the brave kids jumped over that opening. By the time you were eleven or twelve, if you hadn't jumped over that gap you were considered a wimp.

"I remember practicing to see if I could jump the distance. I was pretty sure I could. I measured off where I would start, and how far I had to jump to land safely. It seemed like I had oodles of extra space. I clearly remember, when I finally did it, the powerful adrenaline rush. I jumped the gap frequently after that, taking very short starts and acting nonchalant as hell. Fun!"

I sigh.

"But now I think about what would have happened if I had missed the jump and fallen. I could have really hurt myself. Later, my friends and I would wonder what had motivated this stupid, foolish behavior. Why had we risked crippling ourselves? Things like this only have meaning if you succeed. If you fail, it is stupid, selfish, irrational, crazy behavior.

"If you add something like a skill that has to be mastered—like the kids on their skateboards rather than a kid jumping over a hole—I guess you can rationalize your failures. I don't know, it's kind of fun to think about—but a real bummer if you damage yourself over nonsense.

"But, you know, Silhouette—I wonder if that is the right way to think about it. Rich people can rationalize stupid behavior because they are downhill skiing, but a poor kid can't rationalize his adrenaline highs jumping over dangerous gaps in an unfinished building.

"Okay—enough philosophizing for one night. I'm hungry and tired, and I notice you haven't moved a muscle, so guess you aren't interested."

I turn to Gus. "Mr. Gus-o, are you ready?" He wags his tail. "Well, let's go then—bye-bye, Silhouette."

Gladys

Hi, John. Hello, Bowser. Come for your visit?

Well, tonight I'm in a slightly better mood. Guess it's the weather. Sit, John, sit—let's talk.

I think I mentioned that I was a health care provider—an LPN, actually. That's short for "shit cleaner-upper." That's how I got what I need for my ultimate absence. It's simply amazing how careless hospitals and convalescent facilities can be. A guy in one of the places I worked was caught getting his morphine from the self-administering devices—you know, those automatic syringes that deliver a shot of morphine into the IV tube whenever the patient pushes the happy button.

They measure the amounts, of course, so patients can't OD or stay in a stupor. It seems to be a good system—a patient can give themselves a boost if the oral meds aren't sufficient. In the end, less painkiller is used that way. But to get back to my story—the guy repaired these things, when they broke down or got clogged, or whatever. He'd pick up the device in the patient's room and draw off the excess from the tube, and sometimes take a bit for himself.

It turned out that the dregs didn't satisfy him, so he started sabotaging the units. He made them malfunction more, so he could get more dope. The hospital caught him and wasn't happy, of course.

As I said, I was a nurse—well, you know, a practical. Quarter of a notch up from an orderly, I suppose. Sometimes I liked it—helping people in terrible need. I liked helping the nice ones, at least.

It's interesting—nurses and orderlies talk about how nice people are nice, even when they are suffering. Even the folks with Alzheimer's. Nasty people are even nastier with Alzheimer's, but nice people are nice, even when they are terrified and lost and confused. Bet I'd be a bitch with Alzheimer's! But we'll never find out.

Speaking of which . . . it always baffled me to see strikingly beautiful and smart people—women in particular—so hopeless and depressed and suicidal. Seems like they have everything going for them. Yet some are so fucked-up depressed that they kill themselves. Me, on the other hand? I'm not strikingly anything, but I sure am fucked-up depressed.

Guess there's a message in there somewhere. Maybe beauty is a curse to some women—they feel like vases without flowers. Stupid metaphor, but you get what I mean.

Well, John, I've given up thinking you are ever going to wave to me. Looks like our affair is going to hell. I'd wave, but you'd think I'm more of a nut than I am. For the time being I'll keep having these idiotic conversations with you and Bowser.

I see that Bowser is getting antsy, so I guess you're off again. Maybe I'll see you again. Then again, maybe not. *Au revoir.*

Chapter 10

Jim

I always take Gus on the same route—out the back door of the building where I have a two-bedroom apartment, then down the street to the end of the block. That's a nice walk, especially on a June night like this, when it's still light out. It's quiet and relaxing. Since we're close to the park, it's not unusual to encounter small critters on the way—although Gus is not enthusiastic about chasing them, he watches attentively as the squirrels scamper from tree to tree, and the blackbirds argue in the low branches.

It's cool, and a refreshing breeze gently stirs the leaves. I watch one of the blackbirds, who also seems to be keeping an eye on me, first out of one eye, and then the other. What does he see with the other eye? Probably keeping an eye out for food or his buddies. Maybe he's watching for hawks or other dangers. What eats blackbirds? Raccoons probably like their eggs, and probably the young birds as well. I bet the raccoons think twice about messing with the adults, though. I once saw a couple of blackbirds giving an eagle grief—probably the eagle had been robbing a blackbird nest.

I often ponder the brutality of the food chain. Big stuff eating small stuff. Mean stuff eating gentle stuff. It doesn't seem right or just or righteous. Maybe there's an ironic justice in the cosmos. Humans—who seem powerful and can act mean—get eaten by microbes and cancers, which seem small. Are you reincarnated as a microbe after you have been a human? Would that be an advancement, or would it mean you're starting again close to the bottom, because you've been a bad boy?

A few days ago, I came home and found a pigeon in my bedroom. I'd left the window open, and the pigeon had gotten in and was sitting on the headboard. There was shit all over the place. I used to clean chicken coops when I worked on a farm. It's amazing how much crap comes out of those birds. The crap in my bedroom was like that—it seemed to have come from a flock of pigeons, not just one. After I'd chased the pigeon away, I cleaned up the mess, thinking how nice it was that the peregrine falcons were coming back into the cities to feast on the pigeons.

Some parts of the food chain are more just than others.

"Come on, Gus," I say now. "I'm sure I can find better things to do than to worry about coming back as an intestinal microbe."

We keep walking. The early evening air smells fresh with the odor of newly mown grass. It reminds me of when I played football in my teens. I was pretty good, but only played on local pick-up teams. My high school didn't have a football team, so I never got the chance to see if I was *really* good. But among the neighbourhood teams, I was one of the best. I was big and had a good arm and was accurate with my passes. I liked watching football, too.

"I bet Silhouette does not watch football, Gus," I say. "What do you think? What would we have to watch if we became acquainted? Maybe she would pretend she liked football, just to have our company. Of course, you don't seem overly enthusiastic about football yourself, Gus-o." I thought about it some more. "I bet Silhouette would like to go to concerts. I like that, too. Maybe plays, or the ballet."

A woman approaches, walking her dog. Suddenly I feel awkward, wondering if she heard me talking to Gus. Of course, I speak to Gus routinely during our walks. I also constantly talk to Gus when we're alone in the apartment. That's fine—I just need to be careful when we're out in public. On more than one occasion, I've been embarrassed to discover someone looking doubtfully over at me. I don't want people thinking I'm a fruitcake.

That's one positive thing about my nightly chats with Silhouette. Up to now, they've been mostly silent, in my head. Sometimes I imagine old Gus-o is involved, but he isn't privy to what I'm sharing, really. So, I don't have to worry about anyone walking by and thinking I'm a street person, jabbering to myself.

Of course, sometimes I wonder if I accidentally slip into speaking aloud.

Damn. Why don't I just wave her down and get to know her, and have a sensible, sane relationship?

"I'm just a lonely nutcase, Gus, you know that?"

Gus has relieved his bowels and is waiting for me to clean it up. Taking the plastic bag from my pocket, I bag the feces and drop the bag into a dumpster. I think again about the summer I spent working on a farm, when I was fourteen or so. The farmer said that ninety percent of farming is dealing with shit, and that when farmers go bonkers it's because they can't deal with shit. The manure was everywhere. It took constant vigilance to avoid stepping in it.

Even the dog seemed to shit everywhere. The farmer's wife once said "that darn mutt is made of equal portions of nose and shit." That statement seemed to summarize my life—especially later, when I got into law.

Giggling now, I remember a help wanted ad in the *Globe and Mail*. It was for a position in Manitoba, for a person specializing in "manure management." My farm experience convinced me that manure management was a serious issue, but I could not imagine what the college curriculum must be like for the specialization. I amused myself imagining course titles, such as "Don't Fall in It," "Moving It Around," "Discriminative Mathematical Functions to Know Your Shit," "Methods for Getting Your Shit Together." I wondered if there was a poor slob whose legal specialty was dealing with manure issues. I could see the TV ads: "Is your neighbour not giving you shit? Well, before you speak to anyone, talk to the experts at Manure, Dung, and Pooh. We will get you the shit you deserve."

I giggled again. How about stockbrokers specializing in manure? They'd have TV ads, too: "You too can make it in shit," or "Double your shit, guaranteed."

I decide to move through the remainder of Gus's walk more rapidly. He seems less buoyant, now—tired and hungry and a bit down. He seems down a lot lately, but he still enjoys the meetings with Silhouette. Maybe something would come of the situation. Maybe if I wave, or if she moves a little, we could say hello if we see each other on the street.

Of course, I have no idea what she looks like. I might walk right by her without knowing it. In fact, I've probably already done so.

Chapter 11

Gladys

I need to go to a supermarket. I haven't been out of this apartment for weeks, other than to visit the roof. I have to go out because I have nothing left to eat. I've gone through all the canned goods and packaged foods. I eat infrequently, so my minor stash of storable food had lasted a while, but now it's completely gone.

Maybe now is the ideal time to get on with it—to take the pills. I sit on the edge of my bed, next to the night table where I keep them. I sit there for hours, it seems, trying to work up the courage to do it once and for all. I can't quite get started. I open the bottle several times but always lose the courage to proceed.

I keep having sudden feelings of nausea—shivering and sweating. My bowels loosen every time I think I'm about to do it. I think I need a few more days to make sure that this time I'll do it right. I don't want to wake up again feeling horrible and in absolute despair that I could not even do this simple thing.

So, I decide that I need a few more days. I set the date, make a personal vow, and decide I'll have to get a few things. A last meal.

"What a stupid, idiotic concept," I mumble. The guy in that film *Chamber* wanted Eskimo Bars—chocolate-covered ice cream— before he was gassed. I think they gassed him, before the injection nonsense. Maybe that was a good compromise for him. But I'm not seriously thinking of a final meal. I just need something to eat until I can get it done.

Slowly I get up and walk to my closet. I glance out the bedroom window. It looks a bit chilly outside. I'm always cold, lately, regardless of the temperature. I'll put on a heavy coat. "In my apartment, nausea and loose bowels don't matter much," I say. "But I'll have to make this trip fast, to avoid shitting myself." I'm startled by the sound of my voice, and I start to cry again.

"Damn, damn, damn," I say. "You are such a pathetic, dumb piece of dogshit."

I take my coat, some money off my dresser, and leave the apartment. I lock the door, but I wonder why. I'd welcome a home invasion.

I wonder a lot about God and the hereafter, now that I've committed to taking my life. I remember conversations with my granny about these issues, as I ride down the elevator and start the short walk to the supermarket. Granny went to all sorts of churches. She seemed at home in them all, at least when I went with her.

Granny used to say, "Sweetie, it doesn't matter what you believe about God, as long as you do what's right, and thank God for everything. No one knows anything more than you do about God. Don't be bothered by the gasbags who try to tell you what to believe. They are pompous fakes for trying to tell you that what others believe is sinful, or that people who believe differently should be hurt or killed."

I smile faintly, remembering how Granny used to get "all in lather" whenever she read or heard about "religious fruitcakes" telling people what was sinful, or killing infidels, or other "idiotic self-righteous religious nonsense."

Granny had a friend—a local priest—who she thought was sweet on her. I can't remember what church the priest came from. His name was Father Jacoby, but Granny always called him "David." He was a heavy man, with dark black hair and a round face. Always smiling and laughing. He wore one of those turned collars and a black suit, and his eyes always seemed to be watering. He seemed very nice, but he never paid much attention to me.

Granny and Father Jacoby would sit on the porch, drinking coffee and laughing, talking about the religious rubbish that was forced on children. One of those discussions always stood out in my mind. Its significance only became apparent as I got older. It was about the big bang theory of the creation of the universe.

Enough of that now. I'm approaching the supermarket. Feeling my despair rising and fearing I might lose control of my bowels, I hurry in. I hate shopping here. It's a large chain store. I feel lost inside. Nobody gives a damn who you are or what you're looking for. They just want to sell you expensive food and get you in and out as quickly as possible. It feels wrong and lonely. Of course, when *don't* I feel lonely?

I pick up a basket. I only need a few items. I don't want to buy more than I need, because then I'd have to use it before I "check out." Maybe I'm too incompetent to even kill myself. No—not incompetent, just a coward.

I think that's the first time I allowed myself to use the word *kill* in reference to myself. I wonder about that. Probably has something to do with the Ten Commandments, which spoke about not killing, but nothing about not "checking out."

I stand in the canned goods section, looking over the shelves of beans, the disgusting canned pastas, and the vegetables. But I'm not really paying attention. I'm just standing here, feeling lost.

Jim

I'm meandering down an aisle in the grocery store, looking for canned beans. I need a few cans to hold me over. I dislike this store. It's overpriced, with nothing of interest. It's miserably impersonal.

There's a woman standing in my way. Strange—she's bundled up in what looks like a winter coat, though it's a relatively warm day. She's probably elderly. It seems like old people just feel colder as the grave approaches.

I shudder—what an unsettling thought. I've made a disheartening realization—I'm likely to persist in this state of . . . what is it, exactly? Hopelessness? No, that's not quite right. Fear? Yes, that's closer—I'm just bloody fearful.

"I'm afraid this will go on until the grave," I say.

There are several songs that come back to me when I get into a funk like this. *Is that all there is?* That's a line from one of them. I can hear the tune in my head. The singer goes on to say something about having another drink to deaden the pain.

The second tune has a bittersweet quality. It makes me both hopeful and more disappointed. *Let's close our eyes and have our own paradise*, it goes. I smile. Then the punch line, the key to it all—*Let's fall in love.*

Maudlin, romantic drivel, I think. Let's get back to the canned beans.

Gladys

I'd almost forgotten about the man standing a few feet away from me in the aisle, when he finds the beans he wanted—regular beans with molasses, to zip up his couscous.

"Pardon me," he says, reaching past me to take two cans.

I can barely hear him, but I reflexively turned my head away. I don't want him seeing my face. He doesn't seem to care, in any event. I seem not to have even registered in his thoughts.

I go back to perusing the canned goods. I settle on two small cans of ravioli with garlic tomato sauce. It would be simple and fast, but pretty unhealthy. Ha! But sure, let's be careful about nutrition. Can't kill yourself without proper nutrition, now, can you? Canned ravioli without a vegetable—not good, not good. Maybe I should get some fresh vegetables, go out really healthy. You fucking twit.

Oh, for God's sake—get a can of green beans and get on with it.

Jim

I continue around the store, but I can't stop thinking about my aimless, unrewarding life. I'm a spiritual person, and I want to give thanks to God.

Many years ago, a minister I respected told me that I didn't have to "make a fuss" about praying. A simple "Help me see what you want from me today" in the morning, and a simple "Thank you" at night would do quite nicely. "But," the minister counseled, "every moment of the day just think, 'Thank you, Lord, for this day,' and you will feel much better."

This practice did not seem strange to me. It was similar to what a physical trainer once told me—to strengthen a particular muscle, one should flex or tense it gently every time it came to mind. That way, the muscle is gently tensed up to a hundred times a day.

Anyway, I've adopted the habit of saying "Thank you, Lord" throughout the day. Sometimes I'll add "for this day" or "for this food" or "for what just happened." The latter was for a rewarding experience with a client—or anyone, for that matter. No one knows I do this—I do it inconspicuously. But sometimes I wonder if I really *am* praying.

Prayer is very confusing to me. I have no idea what to say or even if I have to say anything. God probably knows everything anyway. Maybe just being silent and thinking about what I'm grateful for is a gesture of respect, awe, and praise.

The whole praise thing also bothers me. "Praise" is the wrong word. Who the hell am I to "praise" God? There's something judgemental about that. Like a numbskull saying that one piece of art is great and another is lousy. Or what I really thought was just stupid arrogance, when some jerk would say, about someone else, "I think he was quite bright."

Oh well, there I go again. I'm just a bloody "no count," as Uncle Harry used to say, criticizing others for having an opinion. I'm too damn wimpy to even tell someone what I think, except when talking to a woman who does not even seem to know I exist.

I recalled the hymns with the phrase *praise God*.

"Praise God, from whom all blessings flow. Praise Him, all creatures . . ."

I pause. Why *Him*? Why *Her*, for that matter? I think the concept of *Mother Earth* is appropriate. By extension, the giver of life and all things could be thought of as *Her*. But maybe the best idea is to simply always say *God* or *Lord*. Unfortunately, the latter is now used by every two-bit politician, and morons who believe in hereditary excellence.

I snicker. Maybe being alone so much is starting to affect me negatively. I've been seduced by grumbling. I'm not enjoying myself one bit.

Gladys

Ah, fresh produce. I'll select some oranges. But I'll be frugal about it.

How dumb is that! "Don't want to overbuy now, you asshole," I sneer, subvocally.

I remember something an elderly patient once said: "I'm so old I don't even buy green bananas."

Annoyed, I drop three oranges into my basket and walk to the checkout.

Jim

"Thank you, Lord" doesn't seem to be praise—just an expression of gratitude.

What bothers me is the question of whether God cares at all? Is God even aware of me, Jim Paterson? I concluded some time ago that everything hinged on that simple question. Is God personal?

I'm frequently annoyed by people who suggest that their experiences prove the existence of a personal God. Survivors of accidents and the like. "I lived because God saved me!" they say. What rubbish—you survived because you were lucky. Did those who were killed or crippled not have a personal God? Did God choose not to save them? Did God decide that they needed a personal challenge to overcome?

On the other hand, a personal God makes me feel better, so . . . so be it. I had a discussion with an elderly priest some years ago. His counsel was simple. "What you believe will happen, will happen," he said, "so don't sweat it. Believe in a personal God and you will have a personal God, so don't sweat it." I chuckle, remembering the priest's repeated use of that phrase, *Don't sweat it.*

I'm standing in front of the bakery case, staring at the chocolate-chip cookies. I've been lost in my musing—I really enjoy it provided I keep off negative themes. Unfortunately, I have a tendency toward the negative in these philosophical discussions with myself.

I'm a huge fan of chocolate in virtually any form, and I'm particularly partial to chocolate in cookies and ice cream. Try as I might to resist, I usually yield to temptation. Today, I end up with a cookie to eat on my way home. I smile, recalling a T-shirt emblazoned with the statement, "Give me your chocolate and nobody gets hurt!"

Gladys

All the express checkouts have long lines. How annoying. I find a regular checkout with fewer people, purchasing fewer items.

While my items are being rung up by the clerk, I struggle to find my purse in my large shoulder bag. I tense, feeling the annoyance of the clerk and the people behind me.

"Do you have a membership card?" the clerk asks. Members save a certain percentage off the purchase price, and benefit from special "members only" specials. But if I search for my card that will further annoy the people around me. "No," I say.

I belittle myself for my timidity. Then I feel a resurgence of self-loathing—because given my plans, none of this is even slightly important.

Of course, Little Miss Tight-Ass has to save money before doing it. I almost say that aloud.

Jim

I notice the bundled-up woman ahead of me in line, with one person between us. Again, I think she must be one of those elderly folks who is always cold. I glance over at the absurd headlines in the Enquirer.

Chapter 12

Jim

Later, on my evening walk with Gus, I wonder what Silhouette looks like. She seems quite slender. She can't be more than five-and-a-half feet tall. She's probably close to my age. I guess that's to be expected. She probably isn't a knockout, either. Otherwise, why would she be doing what she is doing?

"Well, Gus-o," I say. "I would like her to be my age, with longish blond or brown hair, and nice teeth. Eyes? Oh, probably blue. But I could *really* be excited if she had green eyes."

I once briefly encountered a woman in a bank in . . . it must have been Miami, ten years or so ago. Her eyes were so green and opalescent that they should have been considered lethal weapons. I was transfixed. I could hardly proceed with my banking—I simply could not stop gazing into her eyes. She must have known her power—she smiled so sweetly. She was patient, reminding me that I was in the bank to do banking, and not to act like a klutz looking into her eyes. She didn't put it that way, of course. But I distinctly remember feeling powerless in her presence.

I remember another woman, with grey eyes. She too was mesmerizing, but I can't recall the circumstances. There was nothing sexual about it. It was a long time ago—seems like it was in some office where I was transacting some business. Not a bank. That woman was clearly toying with me—smiling and holding my gaze. I rather liked it.

"But those eyes—my God," I murmur. I fully understand how one can be drawn into and swallowed up by the gaze of another person. The eyes are without a doubt the window to the soul.

Funny how we have this dance with the eyes. Looking at a person for more than a second sets off all sorts of things. On a bus, if two people hold a gaze for a second, there is much awkwardness. I'd try to catch a longer look when I could. I'd long to look into that person's soul. But that's the eye dance with strangers. If you look into their soul, you have to share some emotion—some indication of who you are, and why. I guess that the dance is to sneak a peek into someone's soul without revealing too much of your own. And if the gaze is held longer, we are titillated by glimpses of naked soul.

I see that in day-to-day interactions with clients. I feel profoundly more content about my clients when they can hold my gaze. It shows interest or comfort, or maybe respect. And the feeling is mutual. Such contact makes my relationship with the client was more . . . *bone fide*? But it's more than that, too. I feel . . . friendliness and mutual caring? Perhaps that's too much. I feel content and fulfilled when I can make extended eye contact with clients.

I wonder about people who are uncomfortable making eye contact. Is it because they don't want you to see into their souls? Or because they don't want to catch a glimpse of yours? I kind of feel sorry for them. They seem ashamed of who they are. Autistic kids don't look you in the eye, but I've heard that's because they aren't aware of your presence emotionally—so not looking at your soul sort of made sense in their case.

Fantasizing, I imagine Silhouette maintaining steady eye contact. Her eyes are soft and revealing. Pale blue.

"But wait just a bloody minute, *dummkopf*," I mutter aloud. "What if she's Chinese, or Japanese, or Filipino, or Black, or East Indian, or Native Indian, or Arabic?" I look at Gus, but he doesn't seem interested in my reflections. "Maybe she has black or deep brown eyes, so you can't see the pupils clearly."

I'd had many clients with eyes like that, and as far as I can recall, most if not all made good eye contact. Do I make the same eye contact with eyes whose pupils I cannot easily see? Can they see my soul and I not see theirs? Do I avert my gaze more rapidly with a Chinese woman as compared to one with blue eyes? Maybe I find the steady gaze of black eyes to be more unsettling than, say, those that are blue or hazel or green?

No—I dismiss that idea when I think of the mesmerizing effect of the grey-eyed woman. I remember being clearly unsettled after *that* encounter.

I should do an experiment. I could just make a mental note when gazing at my clients while explaining some legal matter. On a scale of one to ten—where ten was as unsettled as I could ever recall being, and one was trying not to fall asleep—I could rate the women I worked for. I would also have to rate the eye quality—perhaps again on a scale of one to ten, with one indicating I could see the pupil well, and ten indicating the eye was solid black, without a clearly discernible pupil. I once had to do something like that for an introduction service, when I was trying to start a relationship after Sil died.

I couldn't be truly scientific about this, because I couldn't be an objective observer. But it would be interesting to make a mental note of these things. I chuckle. I wonder what the effect of the eyes would be. I've seen beautiful Asian women with jet-black eyes, but

I can't recall if I was able to see into their souls. I was probably too interested in more corporal aspects to be concerned about souls.

What about the myth of Asian inscrutability? Could that be because the window to the soul was obscured, because pale eyes could not discern pupils? It was certainly true that talking to a person wearing dark sunglasses was disconcerting. Is that because the interaction is not equitable? Because the person with sunglasses can see my soul, but I can't see his?

I can't say I feel this way about black eyes. I feel more uncomfortable with sunglasses than with black eyes. I can't say I feel any discomfort at all with black eyes, now that I think about it.

"So, Silhouette," I say. "It is okay if you have black eyes."

There is something extraordinarily beautiful when dark-skinned women have eyes with clearly identified pupils. I remember an ad for perfume or something, in a women's magazine I was thumbing through in my physician's office. A very dark-skinned woman had eyes like a cat. They were light grey with jet-black pupils. I stared at the ad for some time while waiting.

"So, Silhouette," I say again. "It is very definitely okay if you have black eyes, and super-okay if you are Black with grey eyes."

I feel strangely uneasy frolicking with these thoughts. As if praying, I say, "It is definitely okay, whoever you are, my Silhouette."

And your smile . . . in my fantasy, Silhouette always has a smile. A welcoming smile that says, *I wish you well.*

"That's pretty silly," I say. "If she is standing up there hour after hour, she is most likely depressed, or lonely as hell, like me. I bet she has not smiled in weeks. But while she may not be smiling when alone, I bet she smiles radiantly when she meets people. What do you think, Gus-o? Think Silhouette has a radiant, angelic smile?"

Gus doesn't answer.

"Well, it's *my* fantasy," I say, "and I can have her do any bloody thing I want—so smile it is." I sigh, dismissively. "This Silhouette nonsense is turning me into a demented romantic lonely resigned depressed klutz."

We've arrived at the front door of my apartment building—the end of our usual route. I sigh again and we go inside. I'm anticipating another melancholic evening.

The walk had been somewhat longer than usual, and Gus moves hastily to his favourite blanket. The blanket is in front of the bookcase—where the TV is, too. My chair is a few feet from Gus's blanket, facing the TV. Often, I turn the TV on when I feel melancholy, depressed, or just dog-tired. And I certainly feel melancholy this evening. It's a pleasant early summer night. I should be outside, preferably with someone, rather than sitting alone in this stuffy place. Gus-o seems happy snoozing on his blanket, summer night or not. I recall a comment made by an alcoholic friend some years back, to the effect that "no one dies from overexposure to indoor air." Gus certainly embraces that notion. I smile.

"Blast it, Gus-o," I say. "Why am I such a wimpy wimp? What could possibly happen if I waved at Silhouette? No one calls the police because someone waves at them—unless there is a restraining order. She might just decide to stop standing there, if she feels that I am going to be a nuisance." Gus twitched an ear but did not bother to open his eyes. "Maybe she's on the internet—you know, a bloody dating service." I frown. "No, I don't mean dating service. Those are just covers for prostitutes. I think the term is 'introduction service,' or 'mature connections,' or 'harmonious matching services'—something like that."

I had given up on such things. I recall my one adventure with them, several years after Sil's death. I had been whining to a colleague and friend that I was pretty lonely. Well, *whining* might be pretty harsh—I was just sharing my loneliness with someone who seemed to have a friendly concern. He suggested a "connections consultant." I waited a month or so before my friend finally prodded me into making the call. The service was run by two women. They were nice enough, and friendly. They interviewed me for an hour and had me complete silly questionnaires about my likes and dislikes, and what I was looking for in a companion. Details like age, interests, physical attractiveness, personality, and so on. They wanted to know what kind of relationship I was interested in.

How the hell do I know? I remember thinking.

The idea of getting physical with someone scared me at the time. (It still scares me, I admit.) I said something like "I'm looking for a friendship with a lady about my age, maybe a few years younger, who likes music and conversation." The two women asked me if I was interested in a long-term relationship with emotional intimacy—whatever that meant. "I never kiss on the first date," I joked. But the women just smiled and said that for mature adults, particularly those who have been alone for some time, these relationships usually develop slowly.

The consultants connected me with a lady named Judy. Our first phone call was all business, at least for me. I expected to be as nervous as I vaguely remembered being as an adolescent, when I called girls for dates, expecting them to glibly refuse. But I didn't feel any particular anxiety about it—as a lawyer, I frequently made emotionally taxing calls to people.

She was nervous, though—I could tell from her voice, and from her effort to sound cheerful, bright, and clever. Still, she seemed nice enough. We spoke for ten minutes or so, sharing our desire to find some companionship in this lonely fast-paced world, and agreed to meet for coffee on a Saturday afternoon. She recommended a Blenz coffee shop. I do not particularly care for their coffee, but I thought it polite to go along with her suggestion.

"Wonder if that is a character defect in me?" I say to Gus as I pause in my memory. "Always yielding to others' preferences, and then feeling dissatisfied or annoyed at myself for being a wimp." But it was no big deal—just a cup of coffee.

I told Judy that I was tall, that my thinning brown hair had some grey, and that I would be wearing a short green jacket and a floppy fishing hat. Judy described herself as five foot three, and a bit on the "full-figured" side, with greying brown hair as well. She would be wearing a black blouse, black slacks, and some phoney pearls.

We entered Blenz at almost exactly the same time—me from the back side entrance and she from the front door. We saw one another and laughed. *A great start*, I remember thinking. It was nice. We had coffee. I had a cinnamon twist, too. She refused anything but the coffee. I had expected "full-figured" to be a euphemism for "fat and jowly"—but she was just a bit overweight, and not at all unpleasant, physically.

She was very nervous, though, and she had a shrill laugh. I assumed that would soften as we talked, but it didn't. As the afternoon wore on, I began to find it slightly irritating. She took too much effort to laugh at my jokes. We did enjoy talking about our pasts, though—sharing details about who we were and what we did, and the like.

Judy was a receptionist for a car dealership. She spoke of the different salespeople. I was surprised that some of them were women. She described how they had problems with male customers, who thought women could not be knowledgeable about cars. They also had problems with their male customers' wives, who were jealous. After all, the salesladies could talk macho about *torque* and *handling* and such, and the husbands were interested in that.

Judy's boss was the general manager. He was "a real creep who hustled everything in a skirt"—but he left Judy alone because she spoke with his wife daily. "Many of the salesmen were just what one imagines," she said. Judy described the "low-life" finagling to get the most out of the customers. Others, she explained, were just simple family guys trying to get by. They were honest but were always trying to get customers to go for the extra options, because that was how they made better commissions.

One unsavory salesman had a knack for selling expensive cars to intoxicated customers. Men who'd had too much to drink might meander into a car showroom just to look around. This salesman cornered the drunk, persuading him not to pass up the "today only" sale price. Judy described one hilarious situation—the wife of the drunk came back a few hours later, when the showroom was crowded, screaming at the top of her lungs that the dealership was nothing but a "den of crooks who were so lamebrained they couldn't steal unless the mark was drunk." She wanted to "see the scumbag who stole food from her children," because she "was going to stick the contract up his podgy keister."

Judy said that her boss came running to her and frantically asked her to offer the woman a cup of coffee. This suggestion struck Judy as so ridiculous that she asked if she should also offer donuts. She giggled, telling me this story—her boss had damn near fired her on the spot.

I must be snickering to myself as I remember this, because Gus is ambling over now. He puts his head on my knee. I scratch him behind the ear. "Well, old fella—I guess it is time to think of dinner."

Gus becomes more animated at that word. I smile.

"Bet I could teach you to respond to 'dinner' in twelve languages, Gus! Probably more. I'd also wager that if I said 'Harry, come to dinner' you would be happy to comply." I pause to think. "It's strange how mothers have to call their kids to dinner repeatedly before they show up. The problem, Mr. Gus-o, is that they feel this motherly necessity to make sure the brat is fed. They should call them once, and if they don't show, put the food away—problem solved. The shrinks call this 'one-trial learning,' or 'conditioning,' or something. It makes sense. Mother just has to stick to her guns—no-show on first call, no dinner. Now you, my fine slobbery friend—you would never give any mother grief by not coming to dinner. Would you?"

Gus seems uninterested in my musings. "Okay, calm down," I say. "I'm coming—you will get your chow *tout suite*. Here, Clancy—here's your dinner."

Immediately, he begins eating, and I laugh.

"Ah-ha! I win the bet. You have no problem showing up for dinner, regardless of the details of the invitation."

I move to the kitchen to prepare my own meal. I'm a good, fast, and tidy cook, although I don't make anything fancy. During my undergraduate years, I was a short-order cook in a diner. I liked cooking and I loved the job. And I was good at it. I liked all the activity. Many things on the go, at all times. I had to keep track of which orders went together, so a table would all receive their meals at the same time. And I was always cleaning up as I went.

Despite how hectic and noisy it was, everyone had a good time, joking and kibitzing. One of the waitresses, Sally, liked to invent wacky phrases for her orders, like the English "bangers and mash." One was "pigs and clucks looking at you"—fried eggs, sunny-side-up, with sausages. Another was "fry one and leave the moo"—a hamburger cooked medium rare. And "mess 'um with stripes," for scrambled eggs and bacon.

We got into some funny routines over her wacky orders. She liked to come up with orders that I was reluctant to start without asking her for clarification. Her response was always, "Hey, dummy—I thought you were an *experienced* short-order cook." So, I started playing her game—making a guess and starting the cooking. She'd get worried and make some excuse for coming over to my station, glancing at my griddles and stove. It was all great fun.

Then there was Sidney, the dishwasher and philosopher. Sidney had a master's degree. He was brilliant. We'd chat for hours, on profound topics, even during the frenzy of the busy kitchen. Sid must have read twenty books a day. He was the most content person I'd ever encountered.

Sid used to say that if he ever got motivated, he would open a simple fixed-menu truck-stop café on one of the routes that led to the dock warehouses. He maintained that truck drivers were the most knowledgeable folks around, because they listened to late-night radio on long trips. And during his breaks, Sid would have very animated talks with the drivers in the diner. There was one old driver in particular—Wild Bill. He would go toe-to-toe with Sid on some philosophical silliness or other.

There was one heated debate about Pascal's wager, which proved that belief in God just made good sense—being wrong had no negative consequences, but disbelief could be serious. Wild Bill would follow Sid back into the kitchen after his breaks, to continue with the debate. The owner never objected to this comical routine. The two old characters—Wild Bill in his big cowboy hat and the most uncomfortable-looking boots I had ever seen, and Sid in his filthy apron and fez—would be yelling about "Descartes seeking his inspiration ensconced in the pedestrian."

The drivers really took to old Sid. They never said that he should find a job to make better use of his education. But other patrons did. Once, a "suit"—that was Sid's term for the "terminally self-absorbed"—suggested that he should find a "more challenging position, commensurate with his education and intelligence." Sid simply said, "I'm profoundly happy. Are you happy?" Sid radiated contentment. The patron appeared nonplussed, and seemed to whine his answer: "Well, of course."

Sid also tried to get in on my frolicking with Sally. He was Jewish, and liked to call himself "Super Jew, faster than a rolling bagel." He would occasionally order "two supers, with sweet cow," which I eventually learned meant two bagels with cream cheese and strawberry jelly. I scolded him for these attempts, telling him that he was out of his league. "Leave the task of pulling the cook's chain to Sally," I'd tell him. "Stick to something you can handle, like whether or not Descartes took warm baths."

I look over at Gus to update him on my own dinner. "Gus, tonight it's Coney Island couscous," I say. I make couscous routinely. It's healthy, and I can whip it together in a few minutes. "Coney Island" referred to the hot dog that I added as meat for the dish. Hot dogs are unhealthy, but I love the ones I get at a German delicatessen, and I indulge every so often.

I boil the hot dog and broccoli in the same pot until the broccoli is done. I remove the dog and broccoli and save a cup of the liquid. Returning the pot with the cup of liquid to the stove, I stir in a half cup of couscous, turn off the heat, and cover the pot. Five minutes later, I fluff up the couscous and add the broccoli and dog.

"*Voila*," I say to no one. "Fit for a king."

Coney Island couscous can be bland, so I use mayonnaise for the broccoli and mustard for the dog. Normally, when cooking couscous, I add spices and fruit.

I've always wanted to make a short cookbook for lonely people like me. Often, we don't eat properly because we don't have a knack for cooking, or are too depressed to try. We buy prepared meals and nuke them. I loathe the microwave. I've organized sections of this cookbook in my head. For instance: "From Soup to Stews—Starts the Same, Ends Different." Or, for things made of flour: "Griddlecakes, Pot Bread, and Don't Forget the Noodles—It's Just in the Mixing."

When starting with a broth of chicken, beef, or vegetable, I could make anything—from soups to gravies, and from sauces to stews. The differences, I noted for my book, depend only on the thickeners used (corn starch or flour or boiled starches), and what was added (more stuff and thickener for a stew, less for soup, and even less for gravy).

I often ran through a similar "critical path for cooks" for my flour-based array—everything from noodles to bread, and, when sweetened, from crepes to cakes.

I once mentioned my book idea to a psychiatrist, Dr. Haywood. Shortly after Sil's death, friends strongly encouraged me to see someone to help me with my grief and loneliness. My GP recommended Dr. Haywood. He really looked the part—with half-shut baggy eyes, a well-trimmed short beard, and long unruly white hair. He thought that medication was a bad idea, and that it was better to deal with the grief and not simply medicate it away. I agreed, and further agreed to have a few sessions of analytically oriented therapy to help me get on with life.

Dr. Haywood thought that the cookbook was a useful project for me. But he said so in a way that was annoying and condescending. My experience with him proved to be very helpful, but for comical reasons. During the second or third session, I was sitting in the reclined therapy chair, with Dr. Haywood sitting behind and just out of sight. I was talking about things I missed most, now that Sil was gone. Suddenly, I heard snoring.

"Dr. Haywood?" I called softly, turning to face him. "Dr. *Haywood!*"

He stirred and gradually opened his eyes. "Oh—sorry," he said, smiling. "I tend to nod off from time to time."

"Well, I'm not getting much therapy if you are asleep," I said, with more annoyance than I'd normally allow myself to display.

Unbelievably, he replied, "Oh, on the contrary—I do some of my best work when I'm asleep. However, if you wish, we can estimate the time I was asleep and deduct that from your fee for today's sessions."

I said, "Thank you, but if you do your best work when you nod off, that will not be necessary."

Oddly, I did feel better after that session. Maybe it was due to periodic episodes of almost uncontrollable giggling.

Later I wondered if what Dr. Haywood had actually said was that "some of *the* best work is done when I am asleep." Meaning that the patient could use it as an opportunity to express feelings without interruption or disturbance. In any event, that shrink was loony. I named him "Sigmund Bozo" after that incident. He reminded me of a statement my lawyer friend Smitty once made: "A professional is someone who thinks you need his help."

When Sil was alive, I did much of the cooking, though we were always both in the kitchen for meal preparation and clean-up. I always cooked when we had company—I'd swing into short-order cook mode, handling many things on the go at once. I loved it.

Nowadays, I fantasize that I'm cooking for two. I pay attention to the presentation. My dishes are simple, but impressive. I wonder if indulging this fantasy is unhealthy. I don't know why it would be—certainly I haven't lost my sense of reality. I never set the table as though someone else is dining. Nonetheless, I feel sheepish about it.

Chapter 13

Jim

I reverse Gus's usual route tonight, starting from the front of the building and walking around to the back. Tonight, I want Gus to do his business before sitting down with Silhouette. When Gus has to wait, he is often restless, wanting to sniff out good places.

"Hello there, Silhouette," I murmur when we arrive. "I thought I would get Gus's walk out of the way first tonight, so we could visit more peacefully." I look fondly at my dog. "Gus's a good fellow, and really patient most of the time, but when he has not had the opportunity to do his business, he can get feisty. That's reasonable, of course."

Suddenly, I'm thinking back to my childhood. "It's funny—well, not so funny, actually. But the loss of my dog was a defining moment in my childhood. Now I don't think I could ever be without a dog."

This is kind of a long story. I decide to give Silhouette the short version.

"I have felt completely alone most of my life," I begin. "Loneliness is the most salient memory of my childhood, and my early adulthood as well. I had a brother who died when I was only two years old. I have but the vaguest feeling of him. I have seen pictures, of course, over the years. But they always seemed strange—like I was looking at a relative who lived a hundred years ago. A sense of familiarity, but no feelings of recognition."

He was seven when he died, I tell her. "I remember little snippets of when he must have been present. In one, I am in a striped shirt, playing with a stack of blocks. He knocked them down. There is also a smile—no, a *smirk*. And dark brown hair."

I pause, lost in the memory. Coming back to the present, I glance up. Silhouette is still in her spot.

"Do you know, sweet Silhouette—every time I glance up at the stars, I think of my brother. Not that you can see many stars here in the city. But I think of him as floating around out there, ahead of me. At first, I feel really cold and afraid. But then . . . I don't know. A nice feeling, I guess. That feeling isn't about my brother—who I have no real sentiment about, other than a feeling of loss. It's more like awe—looking at a star that may not even be there anymore. The light of the star takes—what, a million years to get here? It may have gone kaput eons ago and I am just seeing its light."

It's hard to get your head around those numbers. The sheer enormity of it is frightening to me. That's why I feel awe.

I go on. "I think it was our good buddy, Einstein, who said that true spirituality was wonderment about the unfathomable magnificence of the universe. Smart lad, that Einstein! I remember how enraptured I was when I learned about his experiment showing the mass of light. I was, I think, in a freshman physics class. These days, I guess every high school student knows about this. But it sure got to me in university. During a total eclipse, you can observe the starlight because the sunlight is blocked. Can you imagine the sheer genius of showing that the starlight was displaced when it passed close to the sun?

"I was dazzled by how Einstein thought this through—realizing that he needed to observe light passing through a substantial gravitational field, to see if there was an influence. Brilliant, just bloody brilliant. Theoretical physics—now that's a field I'd be interested in if I could start over."

I pause.

"Where the hell was I? Blabbering away here. I was telling you about my childhood and got waylaid by the unfathomable magnificence of the universe. Millions of galaxies, and we ask the idiotic question, 'Is there life out there?' Of course there is! Probably billions of civilizations! And maybe God's experimentation with mammals that walk, talk, and use tools has gone better in one of them."

I hope I'm not boring my Silhouette.

"Do you wonder if God is experimenting?" I ask. "Certainly, the ancients thought the gods were having fun, seeing how civilizations would self-destruct because of greed or love. Just think how high-ranking officers on opposite sides speak about each other—you would think that Rommel, Montgomery, and Eisenhower were frat brothers. And in a way, I guess they were. As long as they played by the rules of war, they loved one another. You can't have a war without guys willing to take the other side, now, can you?

"I once had a brief association with a Mennonite minister—I *think* they're called ministers. He described to me what it was like to be a pacifist. He said simply that violence was never justified—even if you were attacked. He avoided any activity that could in any way make violence more likely. So he would not work in arms or defense-related industries—period. A conscientious objector could not even mail a letter for the military, or work for a company that supplied a base with toilet paper.

"He was dead serious. I said—I'm afraid a bit sardonically—that pacifism didn't do the Jews much good in the camps. 'Don't be so sure,' he said."

Was I getting too philosophical? Perhaps, but I decided to press on.

"I think a lot about God. Do you? Atheism makes no sense to me at all. The arrogance of it boggles my mind. The utter complexity of everything—from the universe to the bacterium—is so beyond the human capacity to comprehend that proselytizing in opposition to a superior intelligence is just dumb. Come to think of it, I read the other day about some theory of the quantum physics guys, about the emergence of observer intelligence in the universe, and the potential for that intelligence to be malevolent. Bloody interesting stuff. Agnosticism is a step up, I think—at least those galoots admit their ignorance, pledging to wait and see.

"As for me, I'm devoted to my befuddlement! I love to go to all kinds of religious services. The Catholics and the Anglicans with their incense, and their 'Hail Mary, full of grace, blessed art thou among women,' and their wonderful Gregorian chants. The liberal Protestants with their reasonable and pedantic sermons and bloody good hymns. The gospel churches, Black and white, with their frenetic preachers, and music that makes everyone high. The Quakers with their blessed silence—boy do I love sitting in absolute silence with those folks. And synagogues with the minor keys of the cantor, and the enthralling wit of the rabbi."

I'm reminded of a restaurant I recently visited. "There was a woman singing in the kitchen," I say. "Turned out she was Muslim. A person in the restaurant asked her about her singing—which, by the way, was remarkably beautiful. She said she was singing praises of God—practicing what she would later sing in her mosque. The patron asked if she would be welcome in the mosque, given that she was not Muslim. The Muslim lady said she would be most welcome. So maybe I'll visit a mosque someday.

"It's funny how when you have no first-hand knowledge of something, your impressions can be warped. For some reason, I never associated mosques with music, and certainly not with women singing. But I have never been in a mosque—never even near one—except once, as a tourist. That was a kind of rubbernecking. And it was a very old mosque, and there were no services. (I wonder if that is the correct term: *services?*) In any event, there was nothing going on in the mosque when I visited, so I have no idea, other than from television, what might go on in a mosque during religious services. I never thought of women singing in a mosque. In fact, my stereotypical view was that only men go to mosques—to pray, or to listen to an angry cleric. Shows how ignorant we can be about people.

"I have been in Buddhist temples, though. I liked that also."

I pause again. I'm covering a lot of ground tonight. I go on.

"The slaughtering in the name of God," I say. "That, my dear Silhouette, is the true condition of deranged. Can't imagine what God must say to those people when they arrive at Heaven's gates. Maybe God just lets them in. After all, they are out of their minds—at least I think so. But then, I am devoted to my befuddlement—so what do I know?

"I wonder when our light will go out. I am sure it will be a few million years from now, but I wonder who will be watching that, a few million years after the fact. I just can't conceive of a million light years. There is no shortage of empty space. Of course, we don't have to worry too much about our flame going out—we will be long gone before then. Indeed—it's not totally out of the question that we will be gone as a species in our own lifetime, given the greedy, self-absorbed morons minding the store. And when we self-destruct, there won't be any light implications for anyone to watch anyway. We'll just fade away like the dinosaurs. I love that bumper sticker about how we are on the same extinction path as the dinosaurs—*Too much armor, too little brains.*"

What else can I add? "I wonder if cannibalism was a failed experiment as well. There could have been a gene for that, I suppose. Seems that cannibalism might have been a good idea—a way to keep the population in check. There would be no need for funeral parlors, and certainly we would not use up a lot of valuable land with monuments standing over boxes of dust."

I lean over to Gus—whispering, though I'm still unsure if Silhouette has been able to hear the rest of what I've said. "Gus-o, this is just for your ears. But maybe that's the origin of that demeaning phrase, *piece of ass.*"

I turn back to Silhouette. "I'm sorry, Silhouette—my babbling is getting depressing and morbid. Let me return to my story about my childhood. By any objective standard, it was pretty privileged. There was some pleasantness and good times. Yet the overriding memory was of being alone.

"One memory stands out in particular. I'm about eight, sitting on a park bench two blocks or so from my home, alone, in the rain. I have a rubber raincoat on, and I'm there to feed the squirrels. There are no squirrels out in the rain, but I have put some peanuts around the base of a tree, and I am just sitting there. I remember quite vividly the feeling of loneliness as I sat there in the rain."

Nowadays, I muse, a child that age probably wouldn't be allowed to be alone in a park. They would have a chaperone—or, more likely, an adult would advise them against going in the first place, since squirrels are not crazy about collecting nuts in the rain.

"I have other memories like that," I say, "in which the dominant feeling is loneliness or perhaps disappointment—even in a situation that should have been happy. I feel it at social gatherings where I do not know anyone well. I stand in the background and observe others. I try to busy myself to reduce the intense awkwardness. When I do get up the nerve to introduce myself, it seems to work out okay—but I feel anxious and have to force myself to mingle.

"It seems silly, but I am sure this comes from my childhood. I had no experience interacting with people. Or maybe it is something deeper—maybe I lack self-esteem."

I'm struck by this thought and go silent for a bit. This absolute silliness of being afraid to wave at Silhouette is just more of the same, I realize. I make a vow—I will work on my anxiety, and I promise I shall wave at dear Silhouette soon. I only hope that she won't think me klutzy or call the police—or more likely just ignore me and walk away.

No wonder I became a real-estate lawyer. Can you imagine me in a courtroom?

I suppose I could get some therapy or coaching, or something to overcome that fear of speaking publicly, questioning witnesses, and so on. But to be good in court, you really have to be able to think sharply on your feet. Being anxious seriously limits effectiveness. All the trial lawyers I know are pretty capable socially—not wallflowers. They don't give me the impression of having trouble in social gatherings, as I do. My work is shuffling papers around, and when I am called upon to be forceful for a client, it is more like being a paper lion.

Oddly, I do not seem to have a problem with phone calls. I can call pretty well anyone, and be forceful if necessary, without much concern. Probably because I do not have to look at the person—or because I don't have to be looked at.

Some of the trial lawyers who handle criminal cases are flashy-toothed gregarious types. They are front and center in every office-related social gathering. Others may be relatively quiet, like me, but they do not seem to be tortured by having to relate to people. Maybe they have just learned how to handle it better than me.

I decide to tell Silhouette more about my childhood. "I remember sitting alone in our living room after Christmas, dear Silhouette," I say. "I remember looking at the tree with tears welling in my eyes, my vision blurred. Christmas was almost over, and the feeling of warmth and camaraderie was ending.

"You know, I can't even remember being hugged by my parents. Maybe that's an exaggeration, but it sure says something. It's the bloodiest painful memory."

I look at Gus, fondly. "I think I started this long-winded account of what makes Jim tick with a reference to always wanting a dog. I must have been ten or so when I got my first one. Shortly after, it got distemper and died. Actually, I think the dog was put down. In any event, I was pretty broken up.

"I had just gotten out of the bathtub and was drying off when I was told. I started to cry. No one hugged or comforted me." I frown. "This memory really sticks in my head and craw. I was shivering from the cold, wrapped in a towel, crying, and absolutely alone—even though my mother was not two feet away. She might as well have been miles away. I think my father was there as well, but I am not certain.

"I have had discussions with a therapist about this—but not that idiot psychiatrist I mentioned before. It sounds like I've spent my life in therapy, but that's not the case! I've probably had fifteen sessions, all told—four or so with Sigmund Bozo, and the rest with others who have helped with a few things.

"In any event, the consensus is that I may have missed a developmental stage by not being touched and comforted at the right age. I'm sure there is more to my absurd self-reliance and fear of closeness than that—but then again, physical contact is probably pretty critical to a kid. It was an important deficit in my childhood, seems to me. It's all so odd."

It's been a sad discussion, so I decide to balance the bitter with the sweet.

"One of my *fondest* memories of childhood was when I was ten or so. I was down by the ocean, where you can see the ships in the harbor. It was a warm pleasant summer day. I found a rock, big

73

as a lounge chair, and I reclined on it to watch the ships. I felt so peaceful and content.

"While I was lying there, a black rat came over and put a paw on my leg. It surprised but did not startle or frighten me. Although we were at the waterfront, it wasn't one of those big ugly water rats, but a small fellow—about the size of a big hamster. It kept its paw on my leg, motionless, looking at me for a minute or more, and then ran off.

"Funny how that memory sticks as well. I was completely alone, and yet I felt very content and at peace. I remember returning to that spot later and being disappointed that the feeling was not the same. I suppose the rat had something to do with it, but I'm not sure. I'd felt good before the rat arrived. Maybe my feelings of peace and contentment are what attracted it.

"I sometimes get that feeling of contentment when listening to music—particularly when I'm at a concert. When we get to know one another, Silhouette, it will be my pleasure to ask you to accompany me to one of our orchestra's concerts."

It's been a long discussion. I look at Gus, who seems ready to go.

"Well, Gus, enough of this silliness." I get up and look straight at Silhouette. Should I wave? Maybe Silhouette will wave back, or at least move a bit.

But I can't.

"Bye-bye, my little Silhouette. Pleasant dreams."

I sigh, starting off down the street with Gus—even though Gus already had his walk. It's such a beautiful evening. The air is fresh from a slight bay breeze. There's a single strip of fresh-cut grass behind an apartment, and I enjoy the smell. But I wonder why they didn't cut the whole strip. For Pete's sake, how long would it take to do the whole bloody thing? Two minutes? Probably less. Takes them longer to get a straight-cut edge.

I stand there enjoying the smell of the newly mown grass. But I'm saddened by how it looks like a patchwork quilt.

I resume my walk when I see an uneasy woman, with her dog, scurrying past and looking at me suspiciously.

"I've got to stop this, Gus," I say, once she's out of earshot. "They will be throwing the net over me, and Silhouette will testify that I do seem a bit odd." I glance about. "What shall we do tonight, Gus? I'll cook some—let's see. How about couscous and broccoli and beans for a change? We've only had that three times this week. And then I think I will go to a movie. I am getting pretty bored. No offense—just laying around like another Gus. No offense!"

As we continue walking, I think about how I love movies. I strongly prefer to see them on a big screen. I wrack my brain—I can't think of the last time I've been to the movies with someone. Since Sil died, I've done that on probably less than a half-dozen occasions. I remember I called Judy, my arranged date, for coffee, and asked her to a movie. She sounded disappointed—maybe she was hoping for a more upscale date after the initial meeting in the coffee shop. Something like a dinner and concert—or live theatre, even without dinner. Maybe she just wasn't interested in me. She said she was going out of town for several weeks, and that she wanted to "take a rain check."

I never called her again—nor did she call me. She had my number—or could have gotten it from the matchmakers. Funny—it seemed like we were making out okay. But I'll admit I wasn't feeling any romance.

Chapter 14

Gladys

Hi, John.

I'm not much company tonight. Christ! You'd think I could be at least a tiny bit . . . oh, I don't know. *Up?* Or at least not always dragging my ass.

Let me tell you a story, John. It's one that I find kinda nice. It's about my job—you know, LPN. Practical nurse. But I told you that already, didn't I?

An orchestral conductor—I later found out that he was very famous—was a patient of mine at the hospital. "Patient of mine"—heh. It sounds like I think I'm important. Anyway, this conductor—a Japanese man—was recovering from heart surgery. I was fussing around him—making him comfortable and getting him water and things.

I said that I had heard he was a conductor. He asked me if I liked music. I said that I was very fond of music, and he asked me what kind of music I liked. It just so happened that I had been listening to the CBC that morning before work, and they had played something by Ravel. So, I said I liked Ravel. And then I got nervous, because I thought he was going to ask me what Ravel pieces I liked—and, as you might guess, I know zero about Ravel. I couldn't even remember the name of the music I had heard.

But what a sweetheart he was! He must have known I was completely ignorant about music. But rather than make me look like a jerk, he started talking about Ravel—how he was ahead of his time, and not as rigid . . . I think he said something about not composing by formula. It was over my dumb head.

Then he went on about how Ravel influenced Debussy—or maybe it was Debussy influencing Ravel. He thought that Victor Borge was influenced by Debussy. I know Victor Borge, of course, and his very funny piano routines. The conductor asked me if I'd seen the one where he's accompanying an opera singer who suddenly bursts into loud song, and Borge is so startled that he falls off his piano stool. I think everyone has seen that one! I said yes. He said, "You know how Debussy goes from music so soft it is hard to hear, to an abrupt loud section?" I said yes, though in fact I had no idea what he was talking about. He said he is always taken by surprise by those sudden shifts in volume—when he is drifting off to sleep during a quiet period, he is startled by the sudden loudness, just like in Borge's act.

We both laughed.

I said that he must really hate that rap stuff—that it wasn't real music. But he surprised me. He said, "No, dear—it is all music. Rap, soul, be-bop, hip-hop . . . even children's gurgling."

"But those terrible lyrics," I said.

"In music we tell ourselves and the world how we feel, and sometimes the way we feel is not very nice or pleasant," he said. He explained that early rap was angry, mean, demeaning, and violent. Parents really did not listen to the lyrics at first, but simply said that it was terrible and unpleasant noise, and that the performers were talentless. They dismissed it as silly noise. When parents finally paid attention to the words, they were outraged, and some things started to change. The talent improved and commercial pressure cleaned up the act. "But it is all music," he said. "It does what music is supposed to do—give expression to your inner feelings."

He went on to tell me of situations in which parents used the terrible lyrics to teach their children important lessons. For instance: it is bad to talk about hurting people, and to make women and girls feel worthless, and to threaten the police. These parents, he said, taught their kids that repeating these things in song can make us start to feel that way—just as singing hymns over and over makes us feel closer to God.

"But it is all music," he said again. He said that several times so I would get it, I think. But I still think the rap stuff stinks.

He said, "You know you can make music with just a single word or a short phrase for lyrics. And some are very beautiful."

He sang a few lines of a couple of songs—hymns, actually. One was "oh, my God," repeated over and over again. It was beautiful. Another was "amen," over and over—I've definitely heard that before. And one very nice one he said was a "Negro spiritual." It went "fix me Lord, fix me," over and over. He apologized for having a bad voice, but he didn't—I thought it was beautiful. He said that he was influenced by a great musician of our time—Louis Armstrong, who said everyone can sing. I laughed and told him that was great news because I couldn't hold a tune in a basket. He said that there was a difference between singers like us—he was so kind, implying I could sing as well as he could—and true God-given talent. The problem, he said, was that more people thought they had God-given talent than God had actually given out.

It was so nice to listen to this smart man talk about music. He was so kind and gentle, and careful not to make me feel stupid—even when I said stupid things.

I liked nursing this man. I went to see him every day he was in the hospital—though it turned out to be only a couple of days. One time I said it must be wonderful to hear an orchestra play something you have written. Imagine writing something and hearing it the first time with a huge orchestra. It must be a spiritual thing, I said.

He was so—I don't know, *humble* I guess is the word. He said, "It must be magnificent—I wish I had that talent. But you know—the really great ones hear it completely in their head when they are composing." He said that's why Beethoven—or maybe Bach, but in any event one of the really famous ones—could write such magnificent music, even though he was deaf.

I'm sure this conductor must have written some music, but I didn't ask him. He had a small CD player and was always listening to his music. Sometimes he would have me listen to music on his headset. He would joke that I could only listen to short pieces—otherwise the floor nurse would fire me. (She probably would have, the old bitch!)

One thing he let me listen to was by a man from Toronto. He said he loved this short piece, which was called the "Carnival Overture." It was written after the war. The composer was an immigrant who had gotten out of France just ahead of the Nazis. The guy's name was Oskar something, and he is in his nineties now. The overture I listened to was recently performed in Toronto. I guess that would be pretty exciting, too—hearing something still being played by a big orchestra fifty years after you wrote the thing.

The conductor teased me, saying that if big boss nurse came in, he'd tell her I was trying to fix his CD player. Well, the big bitch didn't come in, and I listened to the whole thing—it was only about five minutes, but so beautiful. I got a little tearful. I felt like such a jerk. The music isn't sad—after all, it's called the "Carnival Overture." But tears started running down my cheeks.

That sometimes happens when someone is nice to me—so it probably wasn't the music, but the man being kind that set me off. Anyway, he just smiled and said, "There is something terribly emotional about music." He said that was what the composer of the music I had just heard had said.

I'll bet he conducted that music in Toronto but was too modest to brag about it.

One time he said that I probably knew about Sigmund Freud, since I was in medicine. (*In medicine!* What a compliment that was, since I just clean up and make beds!) He said that Freud was afraid of music, because it made him unpredictably emotional. He feared being made emotional without knowing how or why.

The conductor said Freud did not know how to "enjoy and embrace" his emotions. I liked that phrase.

The conductor was such a nice man. When he left, he gave me a box of candy and a Maurice Ravel CD—see, now I even know his first name. I take care of some pretty special people sometimes. Not that they have to be famous to be special. Some people are just nice. They are nice when sleepy. They are nice when in pain. And they appreciate everything you do for them.

I've seen the opposite, too, of course. Some people are bitchy when things go well—and bitchier when things aren't so good.

Oh, are going now, John? Well, it's been another day of loony tunes. Is it possible that you are crazy, like me? Talking to yourself, instead of to me? I don't remember you sitting down there until recently.

It's just like me to get hooked up with someone as nutty as myself. Oh, well—take care, John.

Chapter 15

Gladys

I've been standing in my spot for almost an hour, hoping that John will come by early. I want to tell him about my misery. I want to understand it, or to accept its senselessness.

My entire day has seemed senseless. When I got up, I got dressed, as I always do in the morning—I never stay in a robe once I'm awake. And like I always do, I turned on the TV, but I couldn't pay attention. I sat and watched it but was lost in my thoughts.

Since my stress leave, I rarely exit the apartment, other than my trips to the roof deck. I go up there several times a day—often standing there for an hour or more, and sometimes for several hours. I used to wonder if I go up there because I want to jump and end it all. But I've concluded that I'm not a jumper, and that I go up there to be alone and look at the distant mountains.

Oh, to be lost in the forests there! How wonderful that would be. Yet when I used to go into the countryside, I'd have an intense feeling of loneliness, and an uneasiness like fear. I remember the magical time I spent with my granny in the woods and fields—picking berries or just taking walks. I could never recapture those feelings of childhood peace and awe. Now I'm just impatient, lonely, discontented . . . and yes, afraid.

I often visit the roof deck at night. I've been watching John for some time—both at night and during the day. At night he can't see me unless there's a full moon, and during the last one, I moved ever so slightly. He must have seen me silhouetted against the full moon. That's when he started "visiting" me regularly.

I haven't eaten anything since yesterday. I drink lots of tea but ran out of milk two days ago. Earlier, glancing at the TV, I saw that some dumb game show was on. I rose from my chair and wandered into the kitchen. My fridge contained a jar of peanut butter, with just a few spoonfuls remaining, and one egg. Noting that I still had two pieces of pita bread, I decided to make a sandwich. The jelly was long gone, so I placed the egg in a pot of water and turned on the stove.

"A peanut-butter-and-egg sandwich," I said. "Probably the healthiest thing I've had all week."

I'm quite a good cook. I learned many things from my granny. I love to make cookies and cakes. But lately my cooking has depressed me, because it reminds me that I'm alone. So now I make simple, fast meals.

The water started to boil. Normally, I'd turn the heat off and let the egg sit in the hot water for five minutes or so. That method gives the perfect cooked, not boiled, egg—with a slightly soft center. But since I was going to slice the egg into my sandwich, I continued to boil for a minute, and then let it sit in the hot water, so the yolk got a bit harder.

Emptying the peanut butter jar, I sliced the egg on top and rolled up the pita bread. Nibbling on my sandwich, I remembered the cans of pasta I had purchased, but was angry because I forgot to buy milk for my tea.

"What am I doing?" I said aloud. "For God's sake, just do it. What possible reason do you have for sitting here, waiting for your date? You're a coward."

I tried listening to music, but everything made me cry. I couldn't read, because I couldn't focus. I had hoped to lose myself in a book, but never got more than a few pages before feeling sick.

I couldn't think of a good reason why I didn't just kill myself, but I couldn't work up the courage. I sat for hours on the edge of my bed, looking at the bottles of medication I intended to use. Once, I started swallowing the pills, only to get nauseous, with a severe urgency to relieve my bowels. That was the only time I tried to carry out my plan.

I'll do it eventually.

I remember the last nasty patient I had to deal with at the hospital. Deloris Fontaine, an elderly woman—one of the most unpleasant human beings I've ever encountered. I'm not sure what was wrong with her, physically. I overheard doctors and nurses discussing various possibilities. But the main thing seemed to be the pancreas.

I had a different diagnosis: Deloris was a self-centered, once-beautiful bitch. Of all the nasty, selfish patients I've known, she took the cake. She never missed an opportunity to complain about what I was doing for her. And every staff member was subjected to the same nastiness. Her physician hated coming to see her, and openly said so to his colleagues. Every time he visited, he had to listen to her complaints about the staff—and after that, she would start on him.

Once, I happened to be in Deloris's room, fixing her bed, when the physician visited. The physician tried to help her understand that having negative thoughts and focusing on "wrongs rather than rights" was a health risk. She retorted that her only health risk was an incompetent staff, and a physician who was not "anticipating her needs." I vividly remember how pompous that sounded.

Granny had advice about nasty people. "Sweetie," she said, "nasty people are afraid that the world might see them as they see themselves. They are mean in order to keep you away, so you can't see them."

Deloris had mean-looking wrinkles around her mouth and eyes. She was constantly scowling, and she seemed painfully tight. When I tried to make her comfortable by straightening her bedsheets and pillows, she always said something mean, like, "I can see why you're not a nurse—can't even get a wrinkle out of a sheet." On another occasion I was told, "This should have been done hours ago—couldn't cut your break short?"

I rarely gave up on patients. Many of the other practicals—and regular nurses as well—would give up on the nasty ones, avoiding them. They'd neglect the call button, coming in only when necessary. The patients would become more difficult, because the staff was ignoring them. And that just made the staff pull away more. I even heard staff make mean statements, like "I hope the bitch croaks," or, "I'd like to piss in her drip."

I often won over these patients by sheer persistence and gentleness. I'd take the patient's hand and say "You feel very cold—you must be in pain or afraid." I'd been instructed—at nursing school and in a two-day church workshop—on the importance of kind touch. The church workshop was more focused on spiritual healing, but both emphasized that touch could help with healing.

I always called difficult patients by their first names, and I tried to see if they were receptive to touch. My first try with Deloris was very unpleasant. "Don't you call me Deloris," she said. "My name is Mrs. Fontaine, and you are little more than a cleaning lady."

"Deloris," I responded. "I need you to be kind to me, so I can be even kinder to you. Let me rub your arms and hands—they feel so cold. Even if you are nasty, I am not going away, so get used to me."

Deloris pulled her hand away, and said, "Call the head nurse—we'll just see about this."

I hesitated, because big bitch, my boss, would have loved to side with this nasty complaining patient. "You want to tell the head nurse that you don't want me to rub your hands and arms?"

Deloris stared at me with her head cocked for a few moments. Then she said, "Oh, all right—if it makes you happy."

I smile now, remembering this episode. I told Deloris that rubbing her hands would make me happy, because helping people feel better made me feel good. Even after the rubdown, Deloris was unthankful. She told me to stop because the rubbing was making her tired. This was how bitter patients typically responded to my attempts to thaw them.

I often tried to get these patients to talk about God or spirituality. They were terrified, I concluded, for the very reasons my granny had suggested so long ago. Their bitter, angry, and hurtful comments were cover-ups. But I was often quite successful at getting them to be a bit less negative and hurtful.

Not so with Deloris. She became a little less hurtful in her remarks to me, but she left the hospital the same spiteful person she had been when she first arrived. It still makes me sad. My attempts to get her to speak of God were received maliciously. "I'm a church-going Christian woman," she'd say. "I know more about God than you ever will."

Through the open door to the rooftop patio, I hear a vacuum cleaner in the hallway below, and it snaps me out of my memory of Deloris. The maintenance people in my building are very good—they clean and vacuum the hallways every few days.

It is strange that the sound of a vacuum cleaner makes me feel uneasy—a mixture of dread and sadness, or maybe loneliness. I never have this reaction when I'm doing the vacuuming myself, only when I hear someone else doing it. I have no idea why. It must have something to do with my childhood, but I can't think of a specific unpleasant association, except that my home was always unpleasant. But there were other common sounds in that unpleasant house. Maybe my reaction means that I have to be careful not to make a mess. Or maybe it refers to my mother cleaning up after I made a mess.

"I'll never figure it out," I say, "unless God . . ."

I stop, feeling a wave of despair.

God has been on my mind a lot lately. I was raised Catholic—which I suspect has something to do with my hesitancy to "just do it." I proclaimed for many years that I was a "recovering Catholic"—but the fear and guilt are in me so deep that they'll always influence me.

"Kill yourself and you go straight to Hell," I say. "Do not pass GO, and do not collect two hundred dollars."

I don't believe that anymore, but the uneasiness won't leave me. I hope that God is all the good things I've heard and read. But I also feel deeply that God has abandoned me. My misery is so complete that I doubt God knows I exist—or does know but doesn't care.

I hated going to church as a child. We had to go to church to be acceptable in our neighborhood. My parents were always angry on Sunday. They were very impatient with both children and usually argued going to church and coming home.

Granny had none of that anger. I don't know whether she was Catholic or Protestant or something else. She would load me into the truck and say, "Let's go to church." Then she'd drive, until she announced, seemingly at random, "There—that looks like a good one."

Granny always seemed to know people in whatever church she decided to visit. She knew when to stand or sit, and she knew many of the hymns by heart. As with the berry picking, I can't recall anyone else being with Granny and I on these excursions. I do recall asking Granny what she prayed for. Her answer was confusing at the time. She said, "I say, 'Thank you, God, bless my little sweetheart, and help me to have passion for my God.'"

"Granny, please forgive me," I say now, as the tears start. "I've let you down—I can't do it. I mean, living."

Should I go inside? It looks like John is not going to keep our date.

"John, John—where the hell art thou?" I say. "I want to tell you more about me. You know—my work in that castle of misery. It makes you stronger, wiser, more compassionate . . . what bullshit. Just fucking . . . well, hello, Mr. John."

He's here. He's here!

"You're late!" I say. "Account for yourself!" I pause, smiling. "Just fuckin' with you, John—I promise I'm not like that. I'm the most understanding and accepting introverted bitch you'll ever meet . . . oh, and I'm compassionate, too. Of course, the way this little fucked-up affair is going, we'll never meet anyway."

I need to tell him.

"Did I tell you . . . oh, of course not. You just arrived. Yesterday was the day I was to do the job. I sat by my bed—I was actually sitting on the floor with my head against the bed, trying to work up the nerve to start swallowing the stuff. It was a pretty nauseating scene, what with me upchucking every few minutes. Just mostly dry fucking heaves. I had everything ready—water and some bread to make it easier. I took a few pills but couldn't keep the shit down.

"I was praying, John—praying that God would stop the vomiting so I could kill myself. And you know what I kept thinking? How small my fucking head is. That's right. I sat with my head in my hands, praying to God to please let me die, and all I could think was that my head is small. I must look like a distorted freak, I thought."

I sigh. Can he even hear me? "Finally, I gave up. I realized that unless I slit my wrists or jumped over this fucking railing, it wasn't going to happen today. I know I can't jump, but I considered the wrists. Still, I'm not as sure about the wrists as I was about the stuff I swiped from the hospital. I got the straight scoop on that—I have enough to kill us both, five times over. Want to come along?" I grin, and then frown. "No, of course you don't—after all, you got old Bowser there.

"Back to the wrists. If you take a really hot bath and keep the wrists under water you can slit the wrists with a razor, and without too much pain. But I just couldn't do it. So, it's back to the meds for me. It's strange how calm I feel now, John. I made a decision about the date again. It will be in the next few days. I'm not going to share the date with you, though."

I pause, considering. "When I was praying, I remembered I didn't leave a note. That's bad. John—although I feel like shit warmed over, I know I have to. The date is set. And I feel numb."

I decide to return to my story about my last days in the Misery Arms Hotel.

"I was going to tell you about the hospital. This is a pretty miserable story, John, so I hope you can stomach it. I should preface it by telling you that this was the experience that sent me over the edge. I just completely broke down, and now I'm on a short-term stress leave. Of course, I was mega-depressed before this episode, so I probably shouldn't have been working in that area anyway.

"Anyway, Jenny was twenty-five. She was a dear, gentle mother of a sweetheart toddler. She had only a few breaths left after losing the battle with a particularly awful cancer. She'd been in and out of the hospital every few days, it seemed, and each time the medical staff was convinced that she would die within a few hours. She fought to get back home, where she wanted to die. Who the hell wants to die in a fucking hospital? This kind soul, like a lot of people, felt that dying in one's home was important.

"Anyway, you know what Jenny wanted? The *only* damn thing she wanted? She wanted to take her daughter to a store to buy her a dress. She wanted to get the dress with her child, to wear on her birthday, which was coming up in a week or so. That's it. She wanted her baby to have the dress she got with her mommy to wear on her birthday. That way the child would have a story about her mommy—something to hold on to. *Before she died, my mommy and I got this dress for me to wear on my birthday.* She'd tell that story until she was ninety fucking years old."

I pause. The memory is overwhelming.

"You guessed the ending, John. Jenny couldn't get out of the hospital—she died there. She didn't get that dress. But you know the most horrible thing? Nobody would sit with her and share her pain, or at least be a witness to it.

"In one of our in-staff training sessions, we learned about being a 'witness' to someone's suffering. People feel comforted when someone just listens and watches them go through their suffering. Sort of like sharing—or 'validating,' I think was the word they used. I've seen this often with patients. If you sit a while, or listen to them express their fears, they feel better, and actually talk about things other than their illness.

"So, I sat with Jenny and witnessed her pain. Although I think 'pain' is the wrong word. The core of her being was tied up into her pleading with the universe to just let her get that dress, so her baby would have that memory. It would have preserved her in her daughter's memories and life. A kind of immortality. The dress would have been dragged out at birthdays and weddings and funerals. And after the daughter met her first love, she'd have her own daughter wear the dress on special occasions.

"But no one could bear the pain of this. They said stupid things, like, 'It will be all right,' and 'We'll buy her a nice dress,' and 'You have to take care of yourself and not worry about the dress,' and 'Do you want me to get the dress for you?' One poor woman—an aunt or something—actually said that it was too bad Jenny hadn't thought to buy the dress earlier. The aunt was horrified when she realized what she had said—she ran out of the room hysterically, mumbling, 'Oh my God, oh my God.' They all thought they were helping. But most of them—Jenny's coward of a doctor included—wanted to get the hell out of there, because they couldn't maintain themselves in that level of honest hurting.

"I didn't know what to do. I was just a shitty practical. I sat and held Jenny's hand, crying like a baby, and looking into her eyes. I couldn't keep my lip from quivering while she told me about her daughter and this last thing she prayed she could do. I didn't know whether to pray for her to get better, or to pray for her to get stronger so she could get the dress. I settled on 'Please, let Jenny go with her child to buy the birthday dress.'

"I had other patients, of course, but I sat with Jenny as long as I could, and I held her hand. Oh my God, the pain. She kept thanking me. I came into work the next morning and she wasn't there anymore. That was it for me. I started bawling and just couldn't stop. So, they sent me home—stress leave."

I pause again.

"John, I can't understand the cruelty of the universe or God. She would have died peacefully if she had just been able to buy her baby that dress. Why was she denied that? Shit, shit, shit! Poor little Jenny. She probably didn't weigh eighty pounds at the end. What a courageous girl. God, I wish I had some of what she had."

It's too much. "I'm going to check myself out. This isn't for me. Bye, John. Tonight, I'm leaving before you—don't have a fucking heart attack."

Chapter 16

Jim

"Hi, Silhouette," I say.

It's a warm and pleasant evening, and I'm looking forward to a longer-than-usual discussion. But first, I'll take Gus on a quick little walk. He can do his business and then I can spend time with Silhouette without him fussing.

What will we talk about? There was a case at the office that might be of interest. But I'm uneasy discussing these cases, since I never violate client privilege. This case was criminal, so even a general overview would violate privilege. The details would be in the news shortly.

Of course, Silhouette can't hear me anyway. And my discussions with her are mostly sub-vocal. Still, not a proper habit to start.

I should tell her about myself. Or maybe I should wait. I don't want to sound whiny. Discussing my childhood would in some fashion be disrespectful to my parents. They were good people— even though my childhood was not pleasant, and even though I'm not as emotionally fit as I should be because of it.

Gus is tugging on the leash and I pick up his feces in the plastic bag. I go to the dumpster to dispose of it and briefly remember my mental frolicking about manure management.

"Can't share that with a lady, Gus," I say. "At least not until we know one another better." I snicker.

I return to the low wall—my usual place to sit with Silhouette. Gus, seeming to sense that this will be a long visit, curls up close to my feet.

"Well, Silhouette," I begin. "I trust your day was pleasant."

I pause, frowning.

"Damn, I wish you'd come down from there. I'm really starting to worry about you. It doesn't make sense for you to just stand there hour after hour. You don't seem to be smoking. And you are not, I presume, the sentry for some Indian tribe, or keeping a watchful eye out for invaders.

"Speaking of Indian tribes, I was having a chat with a woman at work—Lucille is her name. She had just bought a book of Indian legends for her niece. She read a few lines from one—something about the first person created when the world was clothed in green grass and thick forests. There was also a line about the world being peopled with tribes of animals, and they all spoke one language.

"In any event, we got to talking about our distorted view of the early peoples of the world. How we tend to see them as howling savages, when in fact they had pretty tight family and tribal ties. We also seem to disparage them for not having invented the wheel or formed a written language. But I think that the warmth and beauty of sitting around elders, listening to their marvelous stories, must have been spiritually transforming. The great oral histories, passed down over millennia.

"Can you imagine, after the day's work is done, sitting and having an elder lull your imagination into lands of spirits, dancing bears, and animals that transform into humans? And after you have heard the story hundreds of times and know it by heart, it

92

must be like a church liturgy—it must become sacred. The elders raising the children, rewarding them with wonderful stories, while the parents did what must have been life-threatening work to ensure survival.

"Do you wonder how many ADD kids they had? Probably none, without the scourge of TV and video games. Boy, what crap we feed to our children—and our elders as well. How many elders do we have with children hanging on their sleeves begging for a story? What kind of story could I tell after returning to my tepee from a long hunting trip?"

I stop to ponder this for a moment. "I wonder if the returning hunter embellished the story. 'I was slowly creeping along the ridge of the afternoon sun keeping the wind to my face while watching spirit bear. It was not the time for taking spirit bear, but he presented danger to my hunt for spirit deer.'" I smile. "I'm in too much of a rush to be a good storyteller. I'd want to introduce the bear attack and my escape within the next few utterances. I'll bet the hunter back then would have an hour of story before the bear lifted his eyes to notice him.

"In fairness to me, Silhouette, I would probably be a better storyteller if my story was about my real day. What do I know about trying to get lunch without becoming lunch? I think I could drag out a story about my typical day as a real-estate lawyer."

Come to think of it, I've already told her about that young couple buying their first home.

I go on. "Not much drama in my stories, though. Maybe if I was a criminal lawyer or a big corporate wheeler-dealer, I'd have some classy stories. Though I do see some interesting situations in my work, and experience some real emotions—some good, some not so good.

"I think I told you about that elderly couple who were selling their house to 'scale down' for their declining years. They were pretty miserable, you may recall. Well, yesterday a different elderly couple came in. They were transferring their house to their daughter. I'm always uneasy about these things. I guess I've heard many too many stories about children financially raping their elderly parents. This usually takes the form of 'I promised Mommy and Daddy that they could always live in the house and I would take care of them.' But later, they usually add, 'But I'm too stressed with really important work. They would like it better in the nice retirement home that I have located for them.' And then, 'Oh dear, you have no money other than that meager pension and the equity in your house. I guess we'll just have to find something you can afford on government assistance. Isn't it fortunate that you don't own the house anymore so you can get the government assistance?'

"I'm probably exaggerating here, but I have seen some unbelievably abusive situations where adult children have stolen their parents' retirement security. Well, I'm happy to say this seemed different. The daughter kept reviewing the 'what ifs,' with a clear view toward protecting her parents. It was nice to see.

"In any event, the reason I'm relating this story is that the elderly couple seemed so feeble, and yet so capable, because of their reliance on each other. The man had wild white hair that seemed to have been fixed with hairspray. It stuck out all over the place and was pretty long. His wide eyes had the look of someone witnessing something dangerous. He walked like a man who meant business yet was too uncertain on his feet to walk unaided. He had the short rapid steps of a stroke survivor, who walks fast to keep their balance. He held his wife's hand. She scurried beside him, trying to keep up, and to keep her husband from falling flat on his face. Their arms were bent at the elbows, so their forearms stuck out in front.

"During our discussion, the old fellow was sharp as a tack. He helped his wife and daughter understand the details. I was struck by how kind and considerate he was—never condescending, always asking for their opinions and cheerfully explaining any misunderstandings. He must have been a teacher of some sort—probably a bloody good one.

"After it was done, I had the pleasant feeling of having dealt with a healthy family. I caught a glimpse of the three of them walking back toward me after visiting the washrooms. It reminded me of *The Wizard of Oz*. The old fellow was the scarecrow. The daughter was Dorothy, of course. And the wife was the Good Witch from . . . was it the west or the east? I can't remember. They were flying down the hall, with the scarecrow in the lead, the Good Witch holding up one side, and Dorothy, laughing, and holding up the other."

I stop suddenly.

"Holy smoke, Gus—Silhouette is gone!"

When did she leave? I guess I was too absorbed in my story. (I bet that old guy could tell some stories.)

I feel a bit uncomfortable now. I'd barely seen Silhouette move, let alone wave. Now she's gone, and I missed it. Is this a good sign or an ominous one? I'm becoming more concerned about her safety. She must be depressed. Standing that way for long periods seems worrisome.

"But look at you," I say, chiding myself. "She stands, you sit. What the hell is the difference? You talk to yourself as if she is listening—but for all you know, she's up there singing to herself, or composing music. *You're* the worrisome one, you jerk."

I wait for a few more minutes, wondering if any lights will come on as Silhouette enters her apartment. None do, so Gus and I move on.

Chapter 17

Gladys

I've been wishing that my apartment was located so I could catch a glimpse of John without standing on the roof. Alas, my apartment is on the other side of the building from where he usually stands.

I turn on the living room TV and go into the bedroom. Sitting on the edge of my bed I have an urge to cram the pills down my throat and be done with it.

"I'm such a fucking coward," I say. "I'd better not chicken out. Fucking misery—nothing's going to happen for me. You know it . . . why not do it now . . . come on . . . you fucking creep. Ugly fucking piece of shit."

I pull open the nightstand drawer and grab one of the medicine containers. I start to sweat and shiver, and I feel the bile rise in my throat.

"Do it!" I yell. "Do it, you fucking piece of shit! Worthless—nobody can stand to even look at you, you, you . . ."

I grab the plastic container and try to take off the top. It's a child-proof top, and I struggle. "God damn you, you . . ." The top bursts open and the container slips from my hand, spilling the capsules all over the bedroom rug. I burst into tears and curl up on my bed, drawing my knees tight to my chest.

I stay that way for a long time, sobbing until an exhausted sleep overcomes me.

Jim

I'm on the bus for the short ride home from work. I finally get a seat, after standing for ten minutes.

I like to read on planes and trains, but I rarely read on the bus, unless it's a long ride. On the bus, I prefer to observe and daydream, or watch the city and the people.

I always indulge my pet peeve—counting the people on cell phones and those stupid "personal insensitivity trainers." That's what I call the listening devices that people connect to their ears. This morning, only four of the nine people in the back of the bus were using them. That was good. But tonight, the number is higher: eight of the eleven people in the back of the bus.

I catch the eye of an elderly woman. We seem to share a subtle understanding—the kind that happens between people with shared values. I smile. The woman seems to intuit that I'm lamenting the breakdown of human interaction, and she smiles back, politely. After that, we carefully avoid making eye contact, except for an occasional transitory glance.

The woman reminds me of my grandmother. She has short well-groomed white hair and is slight of build. There's a difference, however—the eyes. The brief locking of a gaze lets me see this woman's kind and gentle nature. My grandmother was a cold and complaining person, but the crow's feet at the edges of this woman's eyes are from smiling and joy, rather than interminable scowling and bitterness. This woman, I surmise, is warm and cuddly with her grandchildren. I can tell by her pleasant smile.

I seem to have a unique kinship with elderly people, especially women. Perhaps interactions like the one I just had with the elderly woman on the bus were common for anyone who didn't use those stupid electronic contraptions. But I suspect it's different for me. I'm not elderly, but my behavior is conservative, and therefore assuring and familiar to older people.

This is certainly true at work. Many of my clients are anxious and frightened older people whose lives are distressing. More often than not, they are influenced, harmfully, by "concerned" relatives. I have a special empathy for these worried people. I spend more time with them during routine transactions. Most of that additional time is devoted to casual conversation about the implications of the transactions, and what the future could be like for this person.

I feel like a therapist with these clients. They regularly ask if they can call me with questions or concerns. I always tell them yes, and I do get calls from time to time. Often these elderly clients just want to hear a reassuring voice.

Someone's cell phone rings to the tune of "Hail to the Chief"—another idiotic quirk of the new technology—and I realize I am close to my stop. The kind woman makes eye contact again. I smile and get up to leave the bus. As I wait near the exit, I'm crowded by two men, one on each side, speaking importantly and loudly into their cell phones.

_____

"Where is that no-good, sorry excuse for a mutt?" I call in a friendly voice as I open my front door. Gus comes running, tail wagging. I stoop down and ruffle his ears.

Since engaging a noon-time dog-walking service, I find Gus is not usually frantic to go out when I arrive home. The walking service is quite well-organized. The first day I used it, I watched clandestinely from a distance. There were two walkers and oodles of dogs. One walker waited outside with four groups of dogs on tethers, while the second entered the apartment and brought Gus out. Attaching Gus to one of the groups, the walkers started off toward the park, with batches of white poop bags flapping on their belts.

I really liked how the walkers—both young women in their twenties—seemed to be having fun. They chatted and laughed and scolded the dogs in motherly ways. Gus seemed delighted.

"Well, Gus-o, my fine flea-ridden friend," I say now. "Tonight is the night before the day I like the best—Friday. The day after that, I shall do nothing but rest my weary bones."

I recall something said by a minister at a church service I attended several years ago. This was not one of those frenetic Bible-thumping routines. The music was wonderfully slow gospel—not the frantic fast stuff that seems to have become popular. The minister spoke about what Heaven would be like for those who "repented and followed in the footsteps of the Lord." He went through several possibilities. One stayed with me. It was from an old slave woman, who'd had a severe life of crushing work, and survived it by singing gospel. She believed that in Heaven she would "do nothing forever and forever."

I like doing nothing. For me, "nothing" is sitting in my comfortable chair by the gas fireplace, reading or listening to music. I never do both at the same time—I can't enjoy either if I try to do both. Gus is always on his blanket at my feet, rump toward the fire and face toward me—opening one eye occasionally, just to check on things.

I giggle, remembering another description of Heaven, which I heard in a sermon in a stuffy Protestant church. The minister droned on about what "must" be in Heaven: pine trees blowing in the wind, crashing surf on a blustery day, and Nova Scotia lobster.

"Come on, Gus," I say. "Let's get you fed, and we will go visit Silhouette."

I'm not hungry, just tired. When Gus and I get back, I'll have cheese, an apple, and some pita bread. Sometimes I don't feel like eating. My lack of enthusiasm about food is because of loneliness. I often fantasize that I'm cooking for two—sometimes that makes me more interested in cooking for myself. Tonight, I'll settle on something simple but healthy, which I'll eat while reading or watching the evening news.

"Good evening, my sweet Silhouette," I say when I see her at her usual spot, as Gus and I come out of the apartment building. "Let me take old Gus-o for his walk, so we can sit for a while without hassle."

Chapter 18

Gladys

Where the hell are you going, John? John?

You certainly saw me here. Standing me up? Well, maybe you'll be back after Bowser shits.

Tonight, I was going to whine to you about my stupid life. You know—what makes me tick, or not tick, I guess. My lousy childhood.

I gaze at the distant mountains. I long to go there, and to walk in the valleys. It could be so peaceful. And yet being away from people and the city is not easy for me. I've tried to get away, driving to rural areas and walking in forests or vast fields. The feelings are always the same: lonely, deserted, abandoned, vigilant, fearful, uneasy . . .

"It's so simple," I say. "No one cares if I exist."

I reminisce about therapy with a very nice woman who was sympathetic, but not helpful. She told me what I already knew—feelings have to be shared. "Joy becomes melancholy if we keep it bottled up," she said.

That was certainly true, but the problem is where the hell to find someone who gives a damn. Always the same, always the same. I shake my head.

"I'm such a screwup," I whisper. No one is going to march up to me and sweep me off my feet. Though that seems to be going on all around me.

A few months ago, on my way to work, I saw two bus drivers—a man and a woman—flirting with and teasing one another. It was at a layover point, and the bus drivers were on a break. I was close to the front of the bus, and I overheard their conversation. The guy was standing in the doorway and the girl was in the driver's seat. Passengers were annoyed as they tried to maneuver past the guy to pay the fare and board the bus. He was mooning over her smile—oblivious to the passengers struggling to get on.

"Get out of the way, silly," the driver softly said. The guy moved to the side but never diverted his eyes from hers.

"What do you like to do?" he asked.

The girl said something about walks, movies, skiing, and maybe partying. The guy offered to put together a list of things they could do if she would like to "hang out with me."

"Are you married?" I was startled to hear the girl say. You would think that for things to have advanced to that stage, such basic information had already been determined. But what do I know? Fat chance someone would be that much in a rush over me.

Anyway, the driver tried to shoo the guy, since she had to start her trip. He moved closer to her and whispered something like, "See you next break." The driver replied, "Oh, don't stay around after your shift. I'll catch you again tomorrow."

"I'll be here on your next break," the other insisted, and jumped off the bus, heading for his own.

My bus driver was pretty—on the young side, and rather small to be driving such a big vehicle. She was pleasant, greeting all the people getting onto her bus—unlike the grumpy guys who seem to hate being bus drivers. The latter always seemed to time their departure so as to strand a few frustrated commuters.

I liked to watch the people on the bus as I rode to and from the hospital. I had to take two buses, but the rides were both short, and I usually didn't mind the commute. Both bus stops were close to the start of their routes, so I usually was able to find a seat.

People seemed so very sad, or maybe angry. Some looked hopeless or despairing. When people recognized others on the bus, they sometimes became animated, and would smile and chat. Sometimes they gave a perfunctory smile and moved on with the same look of despair.

I used to get one of the free daily newspapers, but eventually I got bored with them. I tended only to look at my daily horoscope and then leave the newspaper wedged next to my seat when I got off the bus. The horoscopes were never bad, exactly—but they were guardedly unenthusiastic. My sign is Sagittarius, but the other signs didn't make out much better.

I used to compose my own horoscopes during bus rides.

"Go get him, baby, and screw the star locations."

"Co-workers want to see you fuck up, so make their day."

"Your boss is an asshole, but he's in charge. Do what you want and thank him for his courageous management."

"Be careful around relatives. Be careful around relatives. Be careful around relatives. Be careful around relatives. Get the point?"

"You are going to come in contact with a marvellously attractive person who is going to treat you like shit. But be not dismal—they treat everyone like shit."

"Be kind to an old person, and you shall feel blessed by God and considered peculiar by your fellow humans."

Well, hello, John! You've returned. Are you going to sit for a while? Yes! I see that you are settling in for a nice chat.

This is pretty stupid, isn't it? Well, don't dismay—it will soon be discontinued.

What an asshole I am—know what I did today? I had to go out for a while. I haven't been out of this fucking place in weeks, except for a stop at the supermarket. Today, I was walking to the store. I had my coat pulled tight around me and I was feeling cold as hell. I've been feeling cold lately, even though it's not cold out—what with it being June.

So, I was walking along, passing a McDonald's, and there was a man standing there with a cup in his hand. You know—a paper coffee cup. He was looking the other way. Idiot that I was, I wanted to help, so I reached into my coat pocket and pulled out a couple of quarters. I dropped the coins into his cup, and *plop!*—I realized that it had coffee in it.

Holy shit. The guy looked at me, and I felt like I was going to pee in my pants. I felt like a fucking asshole. The guy must have felt insulted as hell—I had fucked up his nearly full cup of coffee.

The man was Black, and I realized what a bigoted piece of shit I was. If the guy had been white, I would have checked out the situation more thoroughly. I would have determined if he was dressed like a bum, or had a bag of junk by his side, or at least had some change in his cup. But since the guy was Black, standing with a cup outside McDonald's, where the panhandlers often stand, I jumped to the conclusion that he was a bum.

But here's the nice part. He was one of those blessed people who I guess saw that my intentions were good, even though my actions showed what a fucking bigot I was. He smiled—no, not just a smile. He laughed, in a way that I found very nice. He said, "Thank you. That was very kind of you. I guess you give often to folks standing here asking for help."

What a nice man—he found a way to help me feel less like the patronizing bigoted asshole that I am. Then he said that he would give the coins to the first homeless person he met.

I was fumbling all over myself, saying that I was sorry, and that I didn't mean to insult him, and that I wasn't thinking. I offered to buy him another cup of coffee, and asked for his forgiveness. I probably kept chattering at him for a while. Eventually he held up his hand and said, "One can never take offense at an act of kindness. Please do not reprimand yourself for acts of kindness, even if they do not go so well."

That's how he spoke—a bit formal and very kind and gentle. He must have been a minister or something. He said, "Good day, and thank you for your kind intentions." And he walked off before I could get him another coffee.

What a fucking jerk I am—I can't even help someone without making them feel bad.

Well, here goes, John—the story of a fucked-up lonely jerk, whose life is a perfect waste of time. I was born at a very young age. That was supposed to be funny! But mostly I remember being sad and frightened. That's probably why I'm so devastated when I see frightened kids in the hospital. Nothing quite as sickening to me as seeing a frightened child. We tell them such fucking lies.

It won't hurt, dear. Dr. Shithead likes little boys and girls and wouldn't hurt you.

I sometimes feel so terrible when I see these scared kids that I sit by them and try to make them feel better. I ask them what they are there for, and whether they're afraid it's going to hurt. Do they find the hospital a scary place? It even *smells* scary, doesn't it? Things like that. Usually, after I hold their little hands or touch their arms for a while, they tell me they are scared—panicked, probably. I try to tell them the truth—that I would be scared, too, but that they have their mommy and sometimes daddy there also. They have a parent to help them be brave even if it does hurt a little.

The mothers are usually wary of me at first, but generally come around when they see how their child responds to me. I seem to get along with frightened children—I guess it doesn't take Sigmund Freud to figure that one out. They sigh and smile a bit, and I get them talking about other things—like their pets, and so forth.

Big bitch—the head nurse, my boss—called me on the carpet for it once. She said that I get too emotionally involved with the patients. She told me in a very snotty way that I needed to be more detached. What she meant is that professionals shouldn't give a shit. Boy—most of the doctors and nurses learned that part of their training pretty well.

"Hey John," I say out loud. "Did you hear about the patient who died in the hospital? He arrived at the Pearly Gates and was being checked in by Saint Peter. There was a bearded guy walking around in a long white robe, with a stethoscope wrapped around his neck. The dead guy asked Saint Peter, 'Who's the guy with the beard and the stethoscope?' Saint Peter said, 'Oh, that's God—he likes to play doctor.'"

Can you hear me, John?

I was told about my "lack of professionalism" on several occasions—but I guess I just can't help feeling bad about the horrible things I see in there. Screw it—that's the way I am, and big bitch can go to hell.

Perhaps she was right in some respects, given that my reaction to Jenny sent me right over the edge. Yet I was depressed and lonely long before I ran into Jenny. Maybe I shouldn't have been working in a hospital in the first place. Maybe things would have turned out better if I had been a secretary, or a file clerk, or a damn bus driver, or . . . God knows what. But it sure turned out shitty for me—my life has been a complete bust. A fucking waste of the sewer system.

It sounds like I'm really down on the doctors and nurses, but there are some that come straight from Heaven. I knew of one surgeon who had to operate on a small child—who was four or five, I think. He had to remove a growth of some kind. It was near the optic nerves—where they connect and cross over. As I heard the story, there was a strong possibility that the nerves would be damaged during the surgery, and the child would be blinded.

106

When the surgeon and the parents first learned that the child's sight had been saved, the surgeon broke down with the parents. They all cried together. Tears of joy and thanks. I get that anytime someone is nice to me. A breakdown at the end of all that fear and worry.

I can't even imagine what that poor surgeon was going through, knowing that one little mistake could blind the child. The stress must have been unbearable. It must be common for a surgeon to break down afterward. I know some who seem like they wouldn't give a shit if they cut off the wrong leg—other than the insurance and reputation implications, of course—but I'll bet a really concerned, humane surgeon cries when things go well, as well as when they go bad.

From what I heard, the parents and the surgeon just looked at each other and burst into tears and then laughter. The parents were all over themselves, thanking the surgeon. I wasn't there when this happened—one of my friends, a real nurse, was in the room at the time and told me about it. And I saw the surgeon shortly after and I distinctly remember he seemed teary.

I didn't want you to get the wrong idea. There are plenty of schmucks in hospitals, but some real angels as well.

Well, back to my dreary life story. The thing that really stands out about me as a kid was that I fucked everything up. I got my pretty dresses dirty. I dropped the dishes. I failed in school. For goodness' sake, I bet I failed Sand Box 101 in nursery school. I was always being screamed at and smacked.

The smacks weren't hard—just enough to let me know to get out of the way, and that I was considered a piece of shit. My parents hated each other, and they both hated me. My sister hated everyone, including me. I can't say I hated anyone. I was just lost and afraid. I desperately wanted my parents to be nice to me. I remember wanting to help all the time and being told to get away.

But my granny. Oh, great God in Heaven—thank you for my granny. She lived in a small town a couple of hours from my home. My grandfather was a plumber. He was killed when a water tank fell off a truck and crushed him. I was very young, and I don't remember much of him, except that he was very thin and wore wire-rimmed glasses, and that he was always doing something, and I always seemed to be in his way. I remember him yelling, "Watch out, for Christ's sake!" I guess he yelled at me a lot.

Anyway, most of my memories are of my granny living in a small apartment over a store that was vacant most of the time. I remember someone selling Christmas trees in there one Christmas. I think there was a clothing store in there for a while as well.

She moved into that apartment after my grandfather was killed. I don't remember much about the house she lived in with my grandfather, other than it was on a highway and the cars at night made a whining noise as they went by.

I don't think my granny liked my parents much. When we went there, she would take me everywhere with her. When she cooked, she had me sit on a stool and help her. I'd set the table and feed her cats. And every time I wasn't looking, she'd sneak up and give me a warm, glorious hug. She'd call me "sweetie."

The best was when we went berry picking. She drove an old truck with a gearshift that made an awful grinding sound. Granny would say, in her shrill voice, "Come on, you rust bucket—move it!"

Blueberries—that's what I most liked to pick. It wasn't the blueberries so much as where we went to pick them. The berry bushes were in a farmer's field. We had to take a dirt road through tall trees. I loved to walk on that road. But I never went too far, so Granny could always hear me if I yelled.

She told me to sing and make noise, so the bears would know I was out for a walk. I never saw any bears, thank goodness. But I'm sure I heard one once, and it really scared me. I heard the loud noises it made in the woods. It sounded like sticks being

108

broken and someone making a big racket moving through the bushes. Granny had told me to yell if I was frightened or saw or heard anything. But when I heard the bear, I was so scared that I stopped and stood still as a telephone pole. Exactly what I shouldn't have done.

After the bear was gone, I was afraid to tell my granny, because she might be mad at how I'd reacted. But I did tell her, and she said that she had done the same thing once—but next time I should remember to yell. She said there was an old goofy bear who ate the berries. She didn't let me wander off again at all that summer when we were berry picking.

I later heard that a little boy had been killed by a bear at a farm in the area. They thought the bear was rabid, because black bears aren't aggressive, as a rule.

There was a creek running through the field, and I liked to play in the water while Granny picked the berries. I still remember the smell of the mint and fresh water, and the trickling sounds, and the birds around the creek. I didn't like the snakes, but Granny said they were harmless, and to just let them be. But when she sensed that I was afraid, she sat with me while I played.

Once, a snake slithered across a rock close to me and Granny, and then waited there, staring at us. Granny started talking to the snake, and had me notice its eyes, tongue, and colors, and I was not at all afraid.

Oh—I picked berries as well. I was pretty good and fast—at least that's what Granny said. When we got home, we spent hours in her kitchen, cleaning and washing the berries. She put some in the fridge to eat fresh, and she froze some others. But the most fun was making the jam. It was pretty easy, the way Granny taught me. You boil them, mash them, and strain them. Then you put in some sugar and pectin and lemon juice. The lemon juice was Granny's secret. Then you pour them into some mason jars and boil again, put on the boiled lids, let cool and . . . presto! Granny's super jam.

I always begged my parents to let me go to Granny's, but eventually the visits became less frequent, and then stopped. I never knew why, until I heard that my granny had died. I haven't been the same since. It feels like I cried for a year when I found out. God, I still miss my granny—the only person who I know really loved me.

I feel the tears coming now. Are you still in your spot, John? Yes. You seem to be talking to Bowser. You must really love that sorry mutt. I always wanted a pet, but my parents wouldn't allow me to have one. Strangely, I never allowed myself to get one either.

I know I've been talking about ending it, John. I tried the other night, but I didn't tell you. I fucked that up—can you imagine? I can't even swallow pills without screwing it up. I couldn't get the top off—then it flew off and the pills spilled all over the floor. I gave up, and cried myself to sleep.

I don't know if I can do it, John. I'm such a fuck-up and a miserable coward. I was close the other night, if the pills hadn't spilled. But I probably would have thrown them up, since I don't remember having eaten all day.

I had a strange dream that night. I was in a long, messy room with huge tables and shelves. The tables and shelves held a huge buffet of food. I was in the center of things—like a guest speaker after a speech. People were around me and I was explaining something. I was tired and restless and hungry. I wasn't annoyed or anxious to get away from the people, but I told them that I was getting some food and I would be back to finish my explanations.

The food at the front end of the buffet had been picked over, but I remember not feeling badly because that was where the salads, vegetables, and cheeses were. I felt like having meat instead. There were many varieties of meat—probably ten kinds of turkey, and even more of chicken. The turkey and chicken didn't look especially inviting, but the other meats looked fresh and untouched. There were many varieties of each. I filled my plate high with steak, roast beef, and sausages—plus a huge slice of ham right over the top.

I remember wondering how I was going to eat from a plate that was piled so high with food. And then I guess I woke up, because I don't recall anything further in the dream.

Oh, wait—yes, I do! A woman was walking behind me, turning off the lights, like she was closing up.

So, Sigmund John, what do you make of that? Beats me, but I'll bet there's a message in that dream. Maybe I'm so screwed up that I can't even enjoy an abundance of food. Or maybe I'm late for the party. Or maybe I was afraid that I would embarrass myself by slobbering food all over myself and everyone around me.

Oh, I don't know. Who knows? Who cares?

Back to my childhood. Thank God for my granny, I was saying. You know—I don't remember being hugged by anyone else. Strange. But I certainly remember Granny's hug. Granny made up for all the hugs I didn't get. She wasn't cheap with the hugs.

My sister visited Granny less often than I did. Unless I was so taken with my granny that I don't remember my sister being there. I'm pretty sure she was not with us on our berry-picking trips. And I don't remember her helping to make jam, either.

I sure got my share of yelling—lots of yelling in our house. My parents were always yelling at each other. That seems to be the major memory of my childhood: my father and mother yelling at each other. And at me, of course. Even when they weren't yelling, I remember being afraid. Afraid they'd start yelling, I guess. Yelling really frightens kids, unless they get so used to it that they ignore it.

I saw that a lot in the hospital. Worn-out mothers yelling at some sullen child who was pushing their buttons. I'm sure these kids got hit in private. That's just fear, though—of not being liked, or loved. Or even fear of being ignored, I guess.

I think that's what I felt. I wanted someone to give a shit. Some shrinks say that kids can push parents to yell and hit so they at least don't feel ignored. Boy, I get that. But I truly don't think that was me. I remember trying not to get yelled at or hit. I think I said before—the hits weren't too forceful. More like pushes to get me out of the way.

I don't remember hiding in my room or going off by myself. I'd just walk around on eggshells, scared all the time.

I think what changed how I felt about myself was an incident when I was trying to help—again. There were some visitors at our house—I can't remember who. I only remember some women in light-colored flower dresses. It must have been summer, because everyone was sitting on the front porch. I was carrying a tray of drinks—five or six glasses of iced tea, maybe. I have no idea how I got to be carrying the tray. I don't remember being asked, and I don't remember helping to pour the drinks, either. But after thinking about this incident for most of my life, I believe that I may have picked up the tray to be helpful.

My mother was on the porch. She was standing—no, actually she was bending over someone, like she was holding a tray of cookies, offering them to one of the guests. I can see her plainly—she was a little off to the side of the front door as I approached with the tray of drinks. I can see the guest's legs and her printed dress, but not her face.

Well, you guessed it. I went ass-over-teakettle, and the drinks crashed and splattered all over the place. I don't know how I fell—probably caught my foot on the rug. I also don't remember if the drinks splattered on anyone. I just remember my mother. She looked at me with indescribable disgust. Then she looked away. She didn't yell. She picked up the things I had dropped, ignoring me as she walked into the kitchen.

I don't remember her looking at me after that. Of course, I'm sure she did. But the feeling I have is that she never saw me again—not till the day she died, twelve years ago.

Well, John—it doesn't take old Siggy to figure that one out, now does it? My therapist—you remember, the nice but useless lady I saw a few times—said that I developed a sense of shame as a result of my experiences with my parents. Shame, she explained, is about who you are. It makes you feel like you don't deserve to breathe. Those core feelings affect every part of your life and are very hard to change. I still feel like a useless piece of shit. I always will.

And honestly, I'm not so sure it isn't true.

Chapter 19

Jim

"I was reading an article about depression today, Silhouette," I say.

I want to be delicate, so I go slowly. "This worries me about you, by the way. The statistics are staggering. According to one study, in which they interviewed people in all walks of life, over ninety percent of us have thought seriously about suicide at some time."

I pause to ponder that. "I cannot believe that is true. I am sure they had a very loose definition. Sure, I've thought about it—but I never had any notion of actually committing suicide. Of course, maybe I will, someday. I still have many years to go—at least I hope so.

"Maybe they asked if you ever *wished* you were dead. I'm sure many people have done that. I did, after Sil's death. But I don't think I was serious. And the feeling didn't last long. Certainly, after my therapy sessions with Dr. Bozo—the one who fell asleep—I laughed so much I couldn't think about much else for several days. In retrospect, I guess Dr. Bozo was a talented psychiatrist. He made me feel a lot better—he got me out of the dumps. I still chuckle when I think of that. It really did the trick.

"Anyway, the article quoted statistics that say about thirty percent of us will experience a major depression—what they call a clinical depression—in our lifetime. I am in the wrong business, Silhouette. Can you imagine? I could get a psychiatrist's degree on the internet for probably less than five hundred dollars. I'm sure I could learn how to fall asleep as patients drone on about their miserable lives. I could hang up a shingle—Dr. Paterson, Super Shrink—and one in three people would need my help!

"I would probably be great at it. I'm such a klutz at dealing with people that hiding behind the patient's couch and snoozing off would probably be my cup of tea. I'd probably have to be careful about snoring like Bozo. On the other hand, Dr. Bozo seems to have figured out how to handle even that little problem. It certainly worked well with me—I actually paid him for a full therapy session while he napped."

I turn to Gus. "Hey, Gus—do fleabags like you get depressed?"

I suddenly realize I've been speaking out loud, and I glance around to be sure no one is listening. I snicker. Passersby might wonder if I'm a dog psychoanalyst.

"Hey, Gus," I whisper. "Now *that* is a first-rate idea. I could get dogs on the couch and snooze off. You wouldn't complain, like humans do. In fact, you'd probably fall asleep as well. Just imagine, Gus-o, dogs arriving in their Rolls-Royces. I'd have my assistant settle them comfortably on the couch, awaiting my therapy. They'd probably be asleep by the time I arrived, so I could just settle in behind them and snooze."

I pause to think about this some more. "That might be too much sleep for me, though. I wonder if it would work if I read silently? I must consult with Dr. Bozo to see if reading silently is as effective as sleeping as a method for doing one's best work. If necessary, I could change my schedule. I could sleep all day doing therapy and stay up all night doing something else. Heck—why not set up a couch in my bedroom and have my assistant quietly switch patients every hour while I sleep? My assistant would not even have to disturb me. She could sit with the sleeping patient and then switch patients every hour, and charge . . . let's see, if I am really good, being genuinely asleep and all . . . oh, let's not be greedy. Let's say two hundred an hour."

I glance up. Silhouette is still there. I glance around again to see if anyone else is around. The neighborhood is deserted. I relax.

I wonder if I spoke publicly to Gus before this silliness with Silhouette. I'll admit I'm uneasy about sitting here each night pretending to be speaking to a woman on a rooftop. It can't be good for my mental health.

This would all resolve itself if I just bloody waved at her, I know.

But for now, I continue the dialogue. "The article on depression cited many well-known people who suffered from it. There was a psychologist in Toronto who wrote about his long battle with it. And William Styron, the author of *Sophie's Choice*. I guess I was surprised because I assume that people with that level of talent just do not get depressed.

"You know *Sophie's Choice*, of course. I have often wondered about that horrible choice. You remember—Sophie, with two small children, appealed to a Nazi officer to let her and her children go, since they were Christian. The Nazi officer told her she could keep one of her two children and the second would be taken from her. And if she failed to make the choice quickly, both children would be taken from her.

"That choice—my Lord. Just so much to ponder in that choice. If she delayed, the Nazi officer would take both of her children from her. She only had seconds to decide. Which one—the boy or the girl? The youngest or the oldest? Why not tell the Nazi officer to go to Hell? Lose both of the children and maybe her life as

116

well. Was the life, post-choice, worth living anyway? Sophie was doomed to a horrible existence because of it. The child she chose would be a permanent patient.

"What about her trying to get free by citing her Christianity? What the hell would I have done under those circumstances? The fact of the matter is no one has any bloody idea what they would have done. And Sophie has no idea why she makes her choice. Neither would I, if I was in that situation. I am sure I would invent a reason, though. What about trying to escape by distancing yourself from the Jews and others who were on their way to slaughter? Do you think you would martyr yourself, Silhouette? I probably wouldn't, but you never know. Sometimes wimps surprise you when the chips are down. But I am sure I would try any weaseling I could to save my own hide.

"In any event, Styron wrote about his depression as well.

"The article mentioned some other famous people, such as Kurt Vonnegut—you know, the author of *Cat's Cradle*. He attempted suicide. And of course, old Papa himself. Hemingway actually did himself in, even after sessions with a psychiatrist who, as I understand it, was supposed to be a superstar. Beautiful women are supposed to be particularly vulnerable to depression—and, I suppose, suicide as well. Although I do not recall that in the article.

"It is paradoxical to me that people can have so much going for them and yet get so down. But you know, Silhouette, if I look at myself, by any objective standard I have everything going for me. I have a good if unexciting job. I am healthy, as far as I know. I do not lack anything like food or a nice place to live. And of course, I have old Gus-o here. With people dying and suffering all over the world, my whining seems pretty silly. Or even arrogant and selfish.

"Honestly, I think that I am depressed because I am such a wimp.

"The great actor Rod Steiger once described serious depression as like 'bad ice cream.' That's an interesting simile. Life should be a bowl of ice cream—sort of like the song, 'Life Is Just a Bowl of Cherries.'

"Silhouette, blast it—I am going to try to meet you. The first step is to wave, of course. Sure, I would make a choice to resist the Nazis—why can't I get the courage to wave? If I don't do something, my Silhouette, I'm afraid that my tombstone will include the epitaph, *Here Lies James Paterson, Quintessential Example of a Life Not Well-Led.*"

I turn to Gus. "Come on, Gus. Time to resume our dreary existence. Bye-bye, Silhouette."

Chapter 20

Jim

"Tonight, tonight . . ."

In my apartment, I sing softly to the *West Side Story* tune. "I'll wave at her tonight. And then everything will be starry bright. Tonight, tonight—she'll wave back to me tonight, and then everything will be all right. Tonight, tonight—I'll see Silhouette tonight . . ."

I stop singing.

"Blast it, Gus. I cannot think of more things to rhyme with *night*. Your master has lost his marbles."

I've made a commitment. I'm going to wave at Silhouette tonight, in the hope of starting a relationship of some kind. I can't go on in this silly fashion. I have to do something to either make this go . . . or go away.

She will undoubtedly think I'm some kind of nutcase. Who the hell waves at someone on top of a building almost a block away? If she was interested in being friendly or neighborly, she would have waved at me ages ago.

It seems like this idiocy has been going on for weeks, but let's see . . . no, it has only been about one week. And now I am in a stupid fantasy relationship with someone who barely moves, or even acknowledges that I exist.

I look at Gus. "You know, Gus, this situation seems like what they describe autism to be." I pause. "No, that's not quite right. I was thinking of the social psychology course I took centuries ago, as an undergraduate. There was a theory about why negative interpersonal relationships are so stable. The theory was called 'autistic hostility,' I think, and it was based on the effects of negative impressions of others.

"Pay attention, Gus. As I recall, if your first impression of someone is negative, then you avoid that person, and never have the opportunity to validate whether your first impression was correct. What I am doing here with Silhouette, Gus-o, is exactly that. But it just so happens that my first impression was positive.

"I was mooned! Gus-o, remember the first time I saw Silhouette? The big blue moon was behind her. That is where her name 'Silhouette' came from, in fact. She was silhouetted by that big bloody moon, and I was enthralled and enraptured and enchanted. That all probably means the same thing, Gus—I was mesmerized.

"So I have a case, not of love, but, let's see . . . of 'autistic adoration.' Yes, that's it. 'Autistic adoration.' I never test the veracity of my adoration because I never come in contact with her."

Gus is fidgeting around my feet. I grab his leash, and he vigorously wags his tail.

"Well, Gus-o, I know you are desperate for a pee, so let's go out to see Silhouette. But mark my word—it is wave night, the first test of my 'autistic adoration.'"

Walking out the back of the apartment building, I'm startled to note that Silhouette is not in her usual spot.

"Gus-o, this does not look good. What has happened to dear Silhouette?"

I take Gus for his walk, telling myself that Silhouette will arrive at her spot by the time we return.

"You know, Gus," I say, "it's probably good that she is late. When we get back and she's there, my waving will indicate that I missed her. It will be kind of an okay opening for a wave. I'll wave immediately when I see her, so I don't get trapped again in my fear and phobia and shyness, and all the bloody reasons I wimp out."

Gladys

Sitting on the edge of my bed, I'm talking to myself, softly.

"This is it," I say. "I'm not going to carry on with this shit. Why bother? It's silly, and stupid, and pathetic, and sick, sick, sick. Standing up there and waiting for some jerk to feel sorry for me, or look at me, or . . . oh, shit, who knows. I'm just stalling. I said today and . . ."

I feel sick and hurt and alone.

My God. Oh God, I don't know what it will be. Please forgive me—I can't do it any longer. There's nothing, nothing. You've forgotten me.

A stain on the rug catches my eye. I tell myself I should clean it up. Then I snicker dismissively.

"Boy, that's really crazy. I'm going to be gone in a few hours and I'm worried about cleaning a fucking spot on the rug. A spot that I have neglected for months."

I remember reading that people getting ready to kill themselves often clean up, do the dishes, change the toilet paper, leave notes for the milkman, fold their clothes, and even empty the glass of water they use to take the drug that kills them.

Talk about fucking crazy. But I guess when you leave this way you want to be tidy, and not be a burden to anyone. Not like the final "fuck you" of jilted lovers and such.

I haven't decided how to leave a suicide note. I recall hearing of an elderly woman who left a note for her niece on the door to her apartment. The note simply said, "Don't come in alone. I'm sorry. Aunt So-and-So."

Jim

We've just returned from Gus's walk. Silhouette still isn't at her spot. I'm sad and worried.

"Something isn't right, Gus." I look at the rooftop, whispering. "Please, Silhouette. Please give me a chance."

I turn to Gus again. "Let's sit for a while, Gus. Maybe she just got delayed or something. I sure hope she is all right. What a jerk I am. I wait all this time, and now . . . who knows?"

I go to the low concrete wall surrounding the raised flower bed where I usually sit when visiting with Silhouette. I look at my watch. She's at least forty-five minutes late.

"Well," I admit. "It's not like we have a date."

Gladys

I feel bile well up in my throat, and I run to the toilet. Kneeling in front of the bowl, I vomit. When I'm done, I softly sob.

"God, I am so sorry that I am such a . . . oh, I don't know. Fuck!" I shudder at that word for some reason. "Oh, God—I can't talk like that. Will you . . . please help me and forgive me? I just can't do it, anymore, God. Dear God—please give me the courage to finish this now.

"Everything says you forgive and love always, and are there for me, and don't punish those in despair. God—I've tried not to hurt people. I've tried to be a kind and good person. I've done many bad and wrong things, but I'm not a cruel or evil person. Why can't people—someone, anyone—love or even like me enough to care that I'm around?"

I'm getting nauseous again from the stench. Reaching up, I flush the toilet. I feel an impulse to stick my head in the bowl—I recall bizarre stories of people drowning themselves by flushing with their head jammed tight against the bottom of the bowl. But those people were probably drunk and passed out, drowning in their own vomit.

"Please Lord," I say. "Let me do this."

I start to get up, but I feel like kneeling there, draped over the bowl. I flush the toilet again. The smell of the chlorinated water swirling in the bowl brings back memories of a swimming pool I once shared with the only person who I thought loved me. So long ago. It had lasted less than six months, but I recall the simple happiness of that relationship.

Holding hands. "Oh, how I miss that," I mumble. I think of the couples I've noticed lately, holding hands. Old couples, gay couples, young guys with older men, older men, young men, women, a Chinese girl and a Black girl, Chinese girls and white guys, mothers and daughters. Even two old ladies with canes—holding hands and wobbling along. And young kids, too. I smile.

Just a few days ago, I saw a Muslim couple—the woman in her burka, and the man laughing and swinging her arm as they walked hand in hand. I had believed that Muslim couples could not or would not hold hands in public, but this couple certainly did.

"What is wrong with me?" I ask. "I'm not beautiful, but I don't think I'm repulsive. Yet nothing goes anywhere. The men around me are courteous and joke with me a bit. But no one asks to spend time with me. Once I asked Morgan if he wanted to join me at a concert, since I had two gratis tickets. He simply said, 'No thanks.' He didn't even bother to give me an excuse!"

I frown.

"And my women friends are losers like me—just lonely, sad, miserable, boring, tragic, pathetic losers." I'm spitting my words out now. "Fat ones," I moan, "quiet ones, big mouths, whiney ones, crazy ones, and mostly, nauseatingly depressed ones, like me. Antidepressants up the wazoo didn't do shit. You have to take enough to become a fu—" I catch myself. "A *damn* zombie. Yeah, mood modulators. Last time around, that stuff couldn't help a fish to swim."

I pull myself up off of the toilet, feeling nauseous again, and unstable on my feet. Grabbing the sink counter, I catch a glimpse of myself in the mirror. I'm repulsed. Sweaty, hair matted, snot running from my nose, raw red eyes, and chalky pallid skin.

I start to sob and resolve to move to the nightstand, where the bottles are. I'll need lots of water. I should have something in my stomach, so I don't throw it all up. Or maybe I could just drown in my vomit.

Slowly and with an intense feeling of nausea, I inch toward the kitchen. Opening the fridge, I remove a large bottle of water. "Nearly full," I murmur. "No—better take the pills with milk to keep them down. Oh, dear God in Heaven, please receive me. I am such a coward. Life frightens me, and I just can't survive. But you know that."

Why do people pray? God should know every damn thing you're thinking or feeling. Why do you have to mumble about it? I'm so confused—it makes no sense to me.

My gut rumbles. I feel I'm going to lose control of my bowels. I wait for the severe urgency to pass. I hope I can make it to the toilet. I start to sweat and shiver. In my terror, I try to calm myself with the thought that it will soon be done.

Feeling I can now get to the toilet, I rush in, pulling at my baggy jeans, and sitting just as my bowels give way. Sobbing, I feel nauseous, utterly despairing that I might throw up.

"Oh, God—what difference can it possibly make? I'll shit all over myself when I'm finally dead, anyway."

My throat burns from the bile, and I feel my heart pound in my ears.

"Dear God—why can't I just die? Please take me now. Please—a heart attack. It must be close."

I'm having trouble breathing, and the stench from the toilet makes me gag. Flushing the toilet, I move to the side of the bathtub. Turning on the water, I wet a washcloth and clean myself. I toss the cloth into the wastebasket.

How should I let people know to get rid of me after I'm dead? I haven't left a note or telephoned anyone. I could be rotting in here for weeks.

"I'll just leave the door ajar," I say. "Someone will eventually show up. Or I could leave a note on my door. The manager will eventually get it." I think again of the old woman leaving a note on her door when she shot herself. In my note to the manager, I could write, "Don't come in alone."

But who cares? In the end, what difference does it make? I'll be long gone, and it'll be finished.

Lifting my head, I notice the edge of the soiled washcloth hanging over the side of the wastebasket. I lean over and pick it up by the edge. Absentmindedly, I start rinsing the cloth in the tub.

"Oh, for God's sake, you asshole," I hiss. "Only you would worry about this. Don't want to leave a mess, do you—you, you . . . oh, shit!"

Holding the washcloth, I start to sob. I feel sick again, but not like I'm going to vomit. This sick feeling is high in my chest—an ache, really. I start to shiver and sweat.

"Oh, shit—get it over with, you miserable worthless . . ."

I turn off the water, wringing out the cloth and draping it over the side of the tub.

"There, Miss Tight-Ass. Now people will say, 'What a nice lady, to clean up and not cause a mess.'"

Getting up, I notice that my panties are a bit soiled. Sneering, I leave my panties and jeans around my calves, and take small steps to the washbasin, where I splash cool water on my face, and then bury it in a towel. Slowly, I raise my eyes to look at myself in the mirror. Tears start to well and I abruptly look away.

I move to the bedroom and slowly remove my jeans and soiled panties. Finding a clean pair in the drawer, I get dressed again.

I'm ready. I feel emotionally and physically numb—almost calm.

Picking up the jeans and soiled panties, I move to the bathroom to put them in the hamper. Standing in the bathroom with the clothes in my hand, I again feel a sense of disgust.

"Stop stalling," I yell. "Put the fu—" I stop myself from using that word again. "Put the *shitty* clothes in the hamper and let them stink and rot and . . . oh, for God's sake they'll just be thrown out anyway, you sickening piece of . . . oh, I don't know."

I sob.

"Come on," I say. "It's okay—let's just get it over with. You'll just drift off to sleep, and then it's over. Peaceful. No more of this. Oh, God—please help me finish this. I'm sorry."

I drop the clothes in the hamper and walk back to the bedroom. I'm numb.

I decide to leave a note in my mailbox, addressed to the mailman. Since it's Sunday, he'll get it tomorrow and notify the police to come and remove me.

Taking a piece of paper from my computer printer, I write: "Dear mailman. The woman in 1001 has killed herself. Please notify the police. Sorry to burden you. Thank you." Folding the paper, I write in huge letters on the front: "MAILMAN: URGENT. PLEASE READ IMMEDIATELY."

Leaving my door open, I wait for the elevator, hoping I won't encounter anyone. I must look repugnant. I'm relieved to see the elevator vacant. I enter and push the button for the lobby. I feel empty—strangely disinterested in the slow decent. The door opens and I stand motionless.

As the elevator door starts to close, I'm startled back to the present and push it back open.

I step out. I see someone across the street.

John.

It's John. I recognize Bowser at his feet. He's down the block from his usual sitting place. Bowser sniffs the grass. John stands with his hands in his pockets, looking down at his feet.

I cannot move. Why this chance sighting? I've been wondering what John actually looks like. Given the distance of our usual meetings, I don't really know. I have fantasized about his looks—especially the color of his eyes. I wonder about his voice, and whether he has an accent. Does he have nice teeth? Is he bald? He always wears a hat.

He seems deep in thought, unmoving for what seems to be a very long time—much longer than one would expect of a man taking his dog for a walk.

I move forward, placing a hand on the front door handle. I might at least get a glimpse of this man. Someone approaches the building, holding the door open for me. I move forward and find myself standing at the top of the steps leading to the sidewalk.

Outside, the sounds and smells are startling, like a radio coming on too loud. I look around, seeing the intense green of the trees, and hearing a few blackbirds making their racket. I walk toward John, wondering how long he'll remain rocking on his heels, fixated on his dog's sniffing.

Then I remember I have the mailman's note in my hand. I stop, staring at it, trying to decide what to do. I start to turn back, then decide against it. I stuff the note into my back pocket, glancing over to John.

Bowser starts to pull on his leash and John aimlessly follows. He walks a few steps until Bowser locates another area of interest and they stop. John raises his head—looking up at the trees, I guess, or maybe looking for me on the roof. I'm suddenly afraid that he'll turn and spot me—but I relax when he turns his gaze toward the dog.

I cross the street and stand where I think I won't be seen. "Oh God," I murmur. "What am I doing?"

I stare at John's back, wondering if he's going to walk away. I take another step, then freeze as he starts to move. He's stretching. He arches his neck a few times and seems to be getting ready to move on.

Bowser looks up and sees me—again, I freeze, thinking John might follow his dog's gaze. But he drops his head again, and I think I notice an ever-so-slight shaking of his head—like he is thinking the word *no*. I feel compelled to move toward him—and I start to, slowly and quietly, as Bowser resumes sniffing the grass.

Jim

I'm in my usual spot. Why isn't Silhouette in hers?

It's been at least an hour beyond the time she's usually here. I realize she's not going to keep our date, and I'm worried. Although she's not always on the roof in the morning, she's always there ahead of me in the evening. Of course, it's only been a week or so since this silliness started. Still, I'm worried.

When she was there, her stillness had an eerie quality to it. Why didn't she wave?

For that matter, why didn't I? Well, I'm painfully awkward in any social situation, and I fear being thought of as a fool or a klutz. But that's stupid. Waving at a person on a roof can hardly be considered klutzy. Then again, maybe she just wanted some peace and quiet. Some klutz waving at her might at least be annoying.

"Damn it," I mutter. "Tonight, I really was committed to waving—and tonight she does not show."

But I'm also worried that her eerie way of standing so still in the same spot for so long was because she was considering jumping. I've been thinking about this fairly regularly over the last few days. I know people who had jumped to their death. The topic comes up quite frequently at the law firm. I have overheard other lawyers talking about insurance and soundness of mind with respect to these violent suicides.

I think again about Johnson, the guy I knew who seemed to be in great spirits, but who got drunk and jumped off his balcony. I also recall a recent newspaper account of a psychiatrist who killed herself on the same evening that she had seen a full roster of patients. She had killed herself with a potent painkiller, used for cancer patients who needed more than the usual stuff. She had not jumped to her death. The thrust of the article was on the lethal potential of the drug—fenta-something—and how doctors were cavalier about prescribing it.

I wonder if Silhouette works in a hospital, or if she is a doctor. Standing like that, she must be sad.

Hell, look at me. I sit here for God knows how long, talking to myself as though she can hear—or as if she even cares. I'm certainly sad and lonely, too—if not downright depressed.

How do they decide whether someone is just bloody lonely, bored, and sad—rather than depressed? There's something about clinical depression versus run-of-the-mill depression.

I remember my bus ride to work this morning. I guess I was sad myself, because I started taking inventory of the people getting on the bus. Some seemed genuinely happy, or at least upbeat. Some seemed down in the dumps. I discovered some curious things. Almost half of the people had those stupid earbuds, listening to their music. *Good God Almighty*, I thought, *we are cultivating a citizenry of unfeeling zombies*. It was like a scene from *Night of the Living Dead*, in which resurrected corpses advanced toward people barricaded in a house.

But the most curious for me was that the people who were glum were alone, and the people who were upbeat were in groups. I didn't count the annoying people on their cellphones—I found their yelling into their devices very distracting. Focusing on those who were alone and not listening to music or jabbering into a cellphone, I felt that they all looked depressed.

I wonder if "clinically depressed" means they are worried that you are going to kill yourself, or just that you are so bloody unhappy that you can't get on with it?

The fact that Silhouette just stands there suggests that she isn't happy.

Some years ago, I had a daily encounter with an old man in a private rest home. The poor fellow would sit in a wheelchair near the front window. He'd wave to me each evening when I passed on my way home from work. I'd wave back, of course. Sometimes I was the first to wave.

It's ironic that I had a waving relationship with that old man but can't develop one with Silhouette. Undoubtedly, the old man initiated the waving—I would not have started the waving but would have averted my glance if I had seen the old man looking at me. No wonder I am alone and unhappy. I'm too damn awkward to even wave at someone.

What if Silhouette kills herself?

Oh, don't be stupid. She doesn't show up one day and suddenly I'm imagining she might kill herself because I didn't wave at her.

She probably doesn't even know I'm here. More likely, she probably doesn't give a rat's ass.

Gus pulls on his leash, bringing me back to the present. I follow him until he finds more interesting grass to sniff, a few feet along. I'm tired of standing, and I stretch. I'm a bit achy from being slumped over my desk all day.

"I wonder if Silhouette is at her spot yet," I say. But I can't see that area of the roof through the trees. I start to worry about her again. The more I think about it, the surer I am that she's a sad little lady. If she jumps, or kills herself some other way, I could never forgive myself. What if I'm too late?

I remind myself of my vow. If I see her again, damn it, I will wave—even if I come across as an industrial-size jerk. If she thinks I'm a jerk, she won't wave back. And even if that happens, at least I'll know that I did what I could to keep her from hurting herself.

I sigh, shaking my head slightly. "Oh, for goodness' sake," I say. "Your fantasies about Silhouette don't mean anything, save that you are a lonely sap."

But I am really concerned. Her stillness frightens me. Fantasy or not, I would feel like hell if she hurt herself and I just stood around, like the big goof that I am.

Gladys

I continue to approach John very quietly. His back is to me. His shoulders are slumped, and his head bowed slightly forward, as he rocks gently on his heels.

I come up close behind him and say, simply, at hardly more than a whisper, "John?"

His back straightens. He stops rocking and grows still.

Jim

I know instantly. I'm overcome with emotion. I can't get a grasp on what I'm feeling. Triumph? Exhilaration? Joy? Sorrow? Fear?

Yes—definitely fear. I'm welling up with tears. I can't catch my breath. I'm so afraid, yet full of anticipation and elation.

For God's sake, don't screw this up.

How long since she spoke? *Turn, you fool!*

Gus looks behind me, tail wagging.

Gladys

What is happening? I am such a dumb stupid fool to have approached him. His name isn't John. He's probably ignoring me, thinking I'm looking for something from him.

Maybe he does know it's me. Sure, that's it—he knows I'm the jerk on the roof, and he's afraid I'm sick. His sitting there these last few nights had nothing to do with me. Of course. I'm just up to my old pathetic self, hoping that someone gives a shit, which clearly they . . .

"Oh," I say softly as he moves.

Chapter 21

Jim & Gladys

Turning slowly, feeling like he is going to throw up or break out sobbing, Jim looks into Gladys's face. "Silhouette," he whispers.

"Oh, yes!" she whispers back. "Silhouette, Silhouette—I love it. Thank you—I prayed that your name for me would be beautiful, and it is! Please don't ever shorten it to Sil."

"I promise," he says. "You will always be my beautiful Silhouette."

"Well, I don't know about beautiful," she offers.

"There will be no more of that, ever," Jim says, firmly.

Startled, she nods ever so slowly, gazing thoughtfully and deeply into his eyes, realizing from the depths of her being that she is now completely safe. She is besieged with fear, joy, relief, hope, and gratitude.

He's crying, she realizes. There are tears in his eyes. *Oh, dear God in Heaven*, she thinks. *Please let me . . . please help me! Thank you, thank you—please don't let me destroy this. My God, a dream.*

"Is your name 'John?'" she asks.

"Close enough—it is Jim. But if you don't mind, I would like to start anew with John."

John realizes that he is deep inside Silhouette's eyes, and he rejoices at what he feels. He refocuses on her face and sees that tears are running down her cheeks, like they are on his. He hesitantly and ever so gently touches the tear running down one cheek.

She slowly lifts her hand and touches his finger. She wants this moment forever.

John cups his hand around Silhouette's. "Can we take Gus for his walk?" he asks.

"I thought his name was 'Bowser,'" Silhouette says, giggling. "At least that's what I named him."

John replies, holding her hand: "I guarantee that he will come to dinner when called by either name."

Epilogue

Silhouette

I tear up often lately, but they are tears of joy. I know I am lucky. While I haven't lost my fear that this will all come crashing down, I allow myself to cherish the joy. I'm grateful to John for the way he obviously cares for me. I'm grateful to God, for all of this.

But I'm terribly confused about what I've been through. Just a few months ago, I was within minutes of ending my life. Has God heard me?

As soon as I start thinking this way, I chide myself. "For God's sake, don't go there, you twit," I say. Then I go into my "thank you mode," as I call it. I plainly repeat, "Thank you, God—for this day, for John, for everything."

I sit on a bench along the seawall near the Burrard Street Bridge. I look at the homes in the floating village at the eastern end of Granville Island. The homes are painted in different colors, just like homes I've seen in Halifax and in St. John's in Newfoundland. I remember the story my granny told me—that the houses were painted in bright colors so they would be more visible to the fishermen at sea.

I love to sit on this bench and wait for John to come home. *Come home*, I think. How I love to repeat that to myself.

Things have moved so rapidly. I love to remember the deciding episode, when John sat me down on a park bench during one of our walks with Gus. He took my hand, and after clearing his throat, gave a speech that I imagined he'd been rehearsing for weeks.

"Look, Silhouette," he said. "I'm just a big oaf who makes an okay living pushing papers around. I'm not very exciting. In fact, I'm probably boring. But I like simple things and I think you do, too. We have a good time together—at least I do. You are the greatest thing that has happened to me. Sorry, that wasn't very eloquent. But I hope you understand that I love you, and I want to be with you permanently. We have only been doing things together for nine weeks, but I'm convinced that this is right, and I want you to know just how I feel. Given our ages I don't think we should waste time. I want to suggest that we just get on with it and move in together. Sorry, that wasn't very eloquent either. The night we made love—I was just plain scared. You were so kind and caring, and you made me feel—I don't know, just manly, I guess."

He paused, then went on.

"Silhouette, I want to tell you about my wife, Silvia. I loved her dearly. I still do, I guess. I know it's stupid, but I feel that she brought us together. It has been about five years since she died. It all happened so suddenly. She was feeling—"

At this point I whispered, "Slow down, my love. This is important and very beautiful, and we have forever."

He smiled and the tension left his face and body as he sighed and eased back on the bench. He continued, more comfortably. "Silvia was feeling tired and worn out for what seemed to be quite a long time. I told you that she was a bookkeeper and had several clients who ran small businesses. She always maintained that the work was not the least bit stressful, maybe because she avoided taking on too many clients. She seemed to like the work, and got along with her clients.

"What was stressful, however, was that she and her sister Glenna were caring for their uncle, who was dying of liver cancer. He was in a palliative care place out in Surrey. She and Glenna shared the visits, the bills, the discussions with the doctors, and so on. Silvia said he was always just a sweetheart of a man. I didn't know him well, but he did seem to be a nice guy. Anyway, watching him die was so draining to Silvia, and Glenna too. Silvia and Glenna got on really well. I still keep in contact with Glenna—she's a very nice person.

"Silvia went to see her doctor on several occasions, and I just don't know what happened. It turned out that Silvia had quite a severe and advanced leukemia. There were other organs involved—I think that was a more serious problem than the leukemia itself. How the doctors could have missed it is beyond me. All that was needed was a simple blood test and I thought they had done all of those. She had been getting more run down, and the doctors were just giving her pep pills and antidepressants. She died just under six months after her diagnosis. I often wonder if Silvia knew all along and just kept it from me until the bitter end when she just couldn't keep going.

"A few weeks before she died, she asked me to make love to her. She was in severe pain, although she did not talk about it— bless her. The doctors explained to me that the pain was not the leukemia but the other organs. Leukemia caused dreadful fatigue, but she was clearly in severe pain, also. She would moan and yell out sometimes when we moved her. To this day I don't know how she could have endured having sex."

By now, John was choking on his words. He stopped to ask if it was okay for him to be talking about this. I answered without hesitation. "I feel so honored and blessed that you love me so much that you can let me be part of your feelings," I said. "Yes, it is okay. It's more than okay—it's a beautiful gift."

John went on. "It took a very long time to move Silvia. I was so fearful of hurting her. I positioned myself so almost none of my weight was on her. While we were making love, she smiled, and I swear she giggled once. When it was over, she said, 'That was so nice.'"

John fought to keep his composure. He was still choking on his words, and tears were streaming down his cheeks. His voice was barely a whisper when he said the words *so nice*.

So nice.

I'm roused from my reverie when Gus becomes interested in a nosy seagull. I check my watch. Still two hours before John comes home. This is my day off—I only work three days a week now, and I'm happy with that schedule. Tonight, it is John's night to cook. I giggle, saying, "Lord, I hope he doesn't make the Coney Island couscous."

CPSIA information can be obtained
at www.ICGtesting.com
Printed in the USA
LVHW110301080422
715626LV00008B/1449

9 798451 441466